Royally
Jacked

How Not to Spend Your Senior Year

BY CAMERON DOKEY

Royally Jacked

BY NIKI BURNHAM

Ripped at the Seams

BY NANCY KRULIK

Royally Jacked

NIKI BURNHAM

Simon Pulse
New York London Toronto Sydney

First Simon Pulse edition January 2004
Text copyright © 2004 by Nicole Burnham Onsi

SIMON PULSE
An imprint of Simon & Schuster
Children's Publishing Division
1230 Avenue of the Americas
New York, NY 10020

Designed by Ann Sullivan
The text of this book was set in Garamond 3.

Manufactured in the United States of America
20 19 18 17 16 15 14 13 12
Library of Congress Control Number 2003110445
ISBN-13: 978-0-689-86668-5
ISBN-10: 0-689-86668-2

For Lynda Sandoval,
the kind of friend who can peer-pressure
me into jumping off a bridge.
Thanks, because it was totally fun.

Acknowledgments

For their culinary expertise and their knowledge of Vienna schools, many thanks to Chuck and Cindy Burnham. Thanks also to Jennifer Haines and Tina Haines, who didn't laugh when I asked about Uncle Kracker, MTV *Cribs*, or tongue piercing, and to Andrea DeJordy, for giving me James Van Der Beek (fictionally speaking) when I needed him.

I am also incredibly grateful to Julia Richardson, my editor at Simon & Schuster, for all her support, and to my fabulous agent, Jenny Bent. You guys rock the house.

And finally, a very special thanks to my family, for telling me to go write when I was tempted to do anything but.

One

Exactly two weeks, one day, and ten hours ago, my mother completely ruined my life. She announced over her usual dinner of Kraft macaroni and cheese (with tomatoes and broccoli bits mixed in—her attempt at being healthy), that she no longer wished to remain married to my dad.

She planned to move in with her new girlfriend, Gabrielle.

Yep. *Girlfriend.*

She went on and on about how it had nothing to do with me, and nothing to do with Dad, so we shouldn't feel the least bit bad about it. She'd simply come to realize that she wasn't the same person on the inside she'd been showing everyone on the outside. Yeah, right.

Needless to say, I have not yet told *my* girlfriends, with whom I have a totally different relationship than my mother has with *her* girlfriend. Or partner. Whatever. I'm not exactly focused on how politically correct I am in describing my mom's bizarro crush. Especially since I can't describe Gabrielle to anyone yet. I can't even deal with telling them about the *divorce,* which—if I actually let myself think about it for more than ten seconds—is crushing in and of itself. I mean, I had no clue. None. Totally oblivious.

And what's worse—my friends will *freak.*

Then they'll treat me all nicey-nice, giving me those sad eyes that say, *We're soooo sorry,* when really they're thrilled to have something scandalous to gossip about while they're ignoring Mr. Davis's weekly lecture about how we're not keeping the lab area clean enough in Honors Chemistry. Or they'll be so horrified by my mother's newly found "lifestyle" that they'll slowly start ignoring me. In tenth grade—at least in Vienna, Virginia—this is the kiss of death. Even worse than not being one of the cool crowd. Which is the type of person I currently am. Not quite cool, that is.

So tonight I'm eating dinner at the table by myself, watching while my mom and dad stand in the kitchen and debate who's going to get the mahogany Henredon sleigh bed and who's getting the twenty-year-old brass bed I refused to have in my room (and that's going to need duct tape to hold it together if anyone decides to get a little action on it).

"Hey, Mom," I finally interrupt. "I know you want the Henredon, but when Gabrielle was here last week, she told me she thought the brass bed was wicked cool."

My mother shoots me the look of death. "Nice try, Valerie, but I don't believe Gabrielle's used the phrase 'wicked cool' in her life."

I deliberately roll my eyes. "She didn't say that exactly. Geez, Mom. I think she said it was . . ." I pretend to struggle for the right phrase, something that will convince her. Given Mom's behavior lately,

I'm betting she'll do anything to make Gabrielle happy. "Shabby chic? Whatever that means. But it was obvious she really liked it."

I shrug, then look back down at the Thai stir-fry my father made for me before my mom showed up at the door with her SUV full of empty boxes and a list of the furniture she wanted to take to her and Gabrielle's new place.

If I'd had to bet which of my parents had coming-out-of-the-closet potential, I'd have put my money—not that I have much—on Dad. Let me state up front that he's no wuss. He drinks beer and watches Vin Diesel and Keanu Reeves movies like a real guy. He goes to the gym every morning before work and has a smokin' set of biceps and pecs. And according to my friends, he's kind of hot. For a dad, at least.

It's just that for one thing, his name is Martin, which sounds pretty gay. There's a guy at school named Martin who's a total flamer. Not that there's anything wrong with that—I have no problem with people being gay. Really I don't. I'm a live-and-let-live type. But Martin's a *friend,* he's not my *parent*. That's where I have the problem.

Aside from the name thing pegging Dad as potential gay material, he's the chief of protocol at the White House, which means he reminds the president and his staff of things like, "Don't invite the Indian ambassador to a hamburger cookout." (The White House guys are always forgetting that one.) Dad can also describe the proper depth to bow to the Japanese prime minister and the trick to eating spaghetti or the oversized hunks of lettuce they always serve at state dinners without making a mess of yourself. He knows how to tie a bow tie without a mirror and can tell you what kind of jacket is appropriate for a morning wedding.

Believe it or not, these are marketable skills.

Oh, and my dad is an awesome cook. Unlike Mom. I'm guessing Gabrielle's going to be cooking for them.

Playing casual, I flick my gaze toward my mom. "I'm just saying that if Gabrielle really likes the brass bed, maybe you could surprise her with it. That's all."

Getting that crap bed would serve them

right for what they did to me and Dad. Especially if it fell apart under them.

Ick. I do *not even* want to think about this.

My mother leans against the granite-topped island in our kitchen—designed entirely by Dad, appliances, cabinets, and all—and crosses her arms over her chest. She gives him the same cold stare I got when I was busted smoking a cigarette behind the high school last year. "I suppose, if the Henredon really means that much to you, I could take the brass bed."

My dad's mouth curls up on one side. "Sacrificing yourself for Gabrielle, Barbara?"

That's about as nasty as my dad ever gets. My mom just huffs out of the kitchen, yelling over her shoulder, "I'm taking the brass bed. And the Waterford table lamp."

"That was my mother's! Take the mandarin lamps from our room instead. You get two that way. Fair enough?"

She's already halfway upstairs. "Fine!"

"And don't forget to take all your self-help books. There are two boxes of them next to the bed."

My dad turns to me, his expression half sad, half angry with my mom. I think he wants to deck her. I guess she's butch enough to take it now.

I know, I know. *So* not PC. But she's the one who hacked off her long, wavy Catherine Zeta-Jones hair so she could look more like Rosie O'Donnell. Not that short hair's bad—it can be sexy. It's just that there's flirty, Dixie Chicks short, and there's what-were-you-thinking short. No forty-five-year-old with a nice, conservative name like Barbara should wear her hair in a buzz cut. Especially when, at least until a couple weeks ago, she used to love going to the salon with me for a girls' afternoon out so we could get our hair and nails done and be pampered like movie stars.

It suddenly hits me that she probably isn't interested in doing those afternoons anymore. Now I'm getting depressed. And this isn't something mom's self-help books address. Not that I'd read them, even if they did. I have no desire to live my life according to Dr. Phil.

"I'm really sorry about all this, Valerie."

I shrug. I'm good at shrugging just

right, so my parents think I really don't give a rip about anything. "It's not like it's your fault, Dad."

At least, I didn't think so. I mean, was Dad not giving Mom enough attention during their marriage? He was always surprising her with romantic gifts and flowers—and he'd even taken her to the White House a few times for dinner—but was he being as protocol-minded with her in private as he was out in public?

I'm guessing not, since that's no excuse for getting an ugly haircut and moving in with a woman named Gabrielle who's ten years younger than you are. But I try not to think about my parents' sex life. Either them together or, as the circumstances are now, them individually. Eee-yuck.

"I don't think it's either of our faults. These things happen." He lowers his voice and adds, "But if you can save the Mottahedeh china from your mother like you did the sleigh bed, I'll make you whatever you want for dinner tomorrow night."

Whoa. I'm not really sure which china is the Mottahedeh, and I'm wondering why Dad thinks he's going to need *any* china—it's not like he's going to be throwing dinner parties like he and Mom used to anytime soon—as if! But this whole begging-me-to-help-him thing is so not my father. Mom really must be knocking him for a loop.

"Even if I want Peking duck?" I ask.

Dad frowns. "You wouldn't like Peking duck."

"But it's hard to make, right?"

"No. Just time consuming." He squints at me for a moment. I think he's trying to ignore the sound of my mother going through the upstairs closets, rooting around for anything Gabrielle might like. I still say he should get a lawyer. Mom's going to run all over him. But he doesn't want a scandal. Wouldn't be proper, and Martin Winslow is all about proper.

Finally he says, "What if I take you out to dinner? Anywhere you choose."

Ni-i-i-ce. "How 'bout the Caucus Room?"

If you're not familiar with D.C., let me tell you that the Caucus Room is not cheap. It's the kind of place all the rich kids from school go with their parents so they can accidentally and on purpose bump into senators, Supreme Court justices, and the like, then brag about it the next day as if these people were their closest family friends and all hot to write them college recommendation letters. I have no idea if the food's any good—it might totally suck—but I've always wanted to find out. Just because.

"Haven't been there in a while," Dad says, tapping his fingers against the gray-and-silver-flecked granite. I can tell he thinks it's funny this is where I want to go. "But if that's where you'd like to dine, then why not? I'm certain I could get a reservation."

I am not believing my luck. I'd still take having my real mom back—the way she was before making her announcement, doctored Kraft dinners and all—over a dinner at the Caucus Room. But if my parents are going to get a divorce no matter what, as Mom informed me in no uncertain terms two weeks, one day, and ten and a half hours ago, and she's determined to spend the rest of her life shacked up with some peppy spandex-wearing blonde eating soyburgers and seaweed, I guess it's as good a consolation as any.

My dad picks up the cordless and dials without having to look up the number. While he's waiting for the restaurant to answer, he asks, "You do know which is the Mottahedeh?"

"The flowery blue-and-silver stuff?" I guess.

"That's the Wedgwood. She can have that. The Mottahedeh has the tobacco leaf pattern in it. Lots of reds, blues, and greens."

I'm still not sure what he's talking about, but I tell him I'll encourage her to take the Wedgwood, if she wants china at all. Honestly, I think she's more focused on the bed thing.

He makes a reservation for Winslow, then grins at me as he hangs up the phone. The kind of odd grin that gives a girl a real scary feeling, like things are going to get even worse.

"This will work out well," Dad says as he helps himself to a plate of stir-fry. "A few things have come up I haven't told you about, and we have a few decisions to make. Dinner out is as good a time to discuss them as any."

At the uncomfortable smile on his face, I'm wondering, what could possibly come up besides my dinner?

"They're going to make you choose," Jules tells me, in a been-there, done-that tone of voice. She's got her hands under her pits to keep warm, since we're huddled behind the Dumpster at Wendy's, where Jules works part-time. It's the only place we can safely sneak a cigarette without getting caught. Not that I'm a real smoker—it's an emergency-situation-only thing. I can't stand for my clothes and hair to reek. But I decided that telling my two closest friends, Julia Jackson, aka Jules, and Christie Toleski, that my parents have announced plans to divorce constitutes an emergency.

Of course, I left out the Gabrielle part. I'll figure out a way to explain her later. And just so they wouldn't think I was totally pathetic, I slipped in the fact Dad is taking me to the Caucus Room. It took me around two seconds to realize telling them about the dinner was a mistake, or at least, mentioning the part about Dad telling me we had some decisions to make.

Christie takes a long drag on her cigarette, which is only, like, the second or third she's ever smoked in her life. She's five-foot-nine and blond with decent-size boobs, plus she's totally smart and athletic, so she doesn't have many emergency situations. She'd be completely popular if she didn't hang out with me, Jules, and the rest of our gang. I'm sure she realizes it, since the snob kids invite her to their parties every so often, but we've been buds since before kindergarten, and I think she worries about being backstabbed by the cool crowd. We'd never do that to her.

"I don't know, Jules," Christie frowns. "Wouldn't both her parents sit her down to discuss it? You know, do the family meeting thing?"

Jules shakes her head. Her parents got divorced when we were in third grade, her mom remarried the next year, and then divorced the guy the summer before we started sixth grade. Her parents then remarried—each other, of all people— when we were in eighth grade. So Jules is kind of an expert on the marriage/divorce thing. "Not to be rude about it, Val, but what other decisions could your dad possibly mean? My guess is that he wants you to live with him, so he's going to take you out, tell you that you have a choice, then give you that look that says he really wants you to choose him."

As the last word leaves her mouth, though, her eyes suddenly bug out, and she starts to bounce, which makes me nervous. I hate when Jules gets bouncy. "Oooh, unless he's seeing someone! Do you think he's seeing someone? Maybe he's trying to hide it by saying you can live where you want, but he'll kinda pressure you to stay with your mom. Just so he can have time alone with his new girlfriend."

I roll my eyes at her. "There's no new girlfriend, Jules." Not in Dad's case at least. But Jules sounds excited about this possibility, and it pisses me off.

She'd better not tell anyone about the divorce. I consider this A-list-only information right now, and Jules and Christie are the only friends on my A list besides Natalie Monschroeder. Natalie got grounded yesterday for dropping out of Girl Scouts without telling her parents, which is why she couldn't make it to Wendy's. But since we all quit Scouts after fifth grade, and her parents wouldn't let her, I figure she's dealing with her own problems right now and doesn't need to hear about my cruddy life.

Jules blows out a puff of smoke and gives me this poor-ignorant-you scowl. "There's almost always a girlfriend involved, Valerie. Otherwise why would they get divorced out of the blue like that?"

I try not to look right at her. If only she knew!

As a car engine revs nearby, Jules glances around the Dumpster to see if anyone is watching us as she talks. You can never be too careful, and none of us wants to get busted with cigarettes again. Our parents would assume we were secret chain smokers and would ground us for the rest of sophomore year.

"I can't see your mom having an affair," Christie says, which makes me cringe inside. "She's the total soccer mom. But you have to admit, your dad's always going to those upscale parties, and he gets to meet tons of famous people at the White House. Maybe one of them hit on him, and your mom thought—"

"Let's just say there's no girlfriend. Okay?"

"Fine," Jules says, but it's obvious she doesn't believe me. And I don't want to clarify by pointing out that my mom is the one asking for the divorce, not my dad.

"So who are you going to choose?" Christie asks. "If that's what dinner is really about."

"I don't know." I hadn't thought about choosing. I know that sounds stupid beyond belief, given that my parents are now going to be living in two different houses, but it just didn't occur to me. I guess, in my gut, I kind of believed my mom would get over it and move back home. Pull an Anne Heche and decide she's not gay after all.

I'm getting way depressed now. Maybe I should have told just Christie, and not Jules. Or kept my stupid mouth shut entirely.

"Your mom's going to get the house,

right?" Jules asks. "The wife always gets the house. It's kind of a rule."

"Um, actually, she's getting an apartment and my dad's going to stay in the house." I really don't want to get into the details with Jules, so I grind what's left of my cigarette against the side of the Dumpster and I lie. "I think she wants to feel independent or something."

"Damn." Jules looks at her watch. "Gotta go. If I'm late coming off break, I'm gonna get fired."

She got in trouble Monday for not cleaning the Frosty machine the right way, so she promised the manager she'd redo it today. She's dying to get moved up to cash register so she doesn't smell like french fry grease at the end of every day.

"Listen, Val," she sniffs, "I'd normally tell you to stay with your mom, but if you're going to lose your bedroom and have to move into some tiny apartment—"

"But how could you not live with your mom?" Christie says in shock. Christie's been coming over to my house since preschool, so she knows my mom pretty well. At least, the way my mom used to be.

"I don't know," I admit. And it's true. I can't imagine not living with Mom. But I feel the same way about Dad. I don't want to not live with either of them.

Jules drops the butt of her cigarette into the snow, then pops two cinnamon Altoids into her mouth and passes the box to me before Christie steals one. "I gotta go. Call me tonight and tell me what happens. 'Kay, Val?"

"It's probably going to be late."

"First thing tomorrow then," she says, tucking the Altoids box back into the pocket of her black polyester Wendy's pants. "But call by nine. It's Saturday, so I'm on the lunch shift."

Once she's crossed the parking lot and ducked into the back door, Christie lets out a painful-sounding sigh. "Don't listen to her, Val. You know how she is."

"Yeah." I give her my "whatever" shrug.

"It'll be okay. And you know I'm here for you if you need me. Anytime, day or night. Just call me," she says, adjusting her hood so her hair is tucked inside.

It kills me how pretty Christie is without even trying. She had one zit—*one*—a couple months ago, and it was very nearly a cigarette-smoking emergency situation, she was so certain her boyfriend would dump her. As if. Over a *zit*? I wanted to smack her back to reality. First, over her lack of zittiness (is that a word?), and second over her boyfriend insecurity. He's totally into her. Still, she could do a lot better than Jeremy Astin, if you ask me. But Christie's way nice, and pretty much my best friend, so I don't want to hurt her feelings by telling her this. She loves Jeremy, even if he is a little too much into cross-country and runs in public wearing those icky nylon shorts, even when it's ice-cold outside.

I'm just about to say good-bye and walk back to school to get my junk out of my locker when I see a familiar green Toyota SUV in the drive-thru. It's my mom and, to my horror, Gabrielle is with her. Why I have no clue, since Gabrielle is a crusader-type vegetarian.

Before I can say something to Christie to keep her from seeing them, she grabs the sleeve of my coat. "I almost forgot to tell you, with Jules here and you telling us about the divorce and all, but Jeremy said that he and David were talking in the library yesterday, and your name came up."

Since I have had a crush on David Anderson since, like, kindergarten, I actually look away from my mom and Gabrielle and pull Christie another step behind the Dumpster.

"Are you serious?" I ask, trying not to sound too excited, even though Christie knows I would just die to go out with him. "Who brought me up, David or Jeremy?"

"David did. He asked Jeremy if you were with anybody."

My heart does an instant flip-flop in my chest. You have got to see David to know why. He's a total, one hundred percent hottie. Surfer-blond, with these fantabulous green eyes I can't even look into, they're so freakin' gorgeous. He could bump Paul Walker or James Van Der Beek right off the cover of *Teen People* and females everywhere would rejoice, I kid you not. Even those who are still whining about *Dawson's Creek* going off the air. And even though he's never asked me out, I think we'd totally gel. I mean, we share a group of friends, we both have parents in politics, and we're hyper about our grades. "What did Jeremy say?"

"He played it cool. Said he didn't think so, but he knew a couple of other guys liked you."

"Wow. Good one." Jeremy just scored major points with this, as long as David didn't catch on to the bluff. Maybe Jeremy does deserve Christie after all. "Then what happened?"

"That was it. But Jeremy definitely got the impression he's interested. Like maybe we could all four go out sometime."

I think I am going to collapse. Right behind the Wendy's Dumpster, snow and old french fry muck and all.

Christie is grinning now, and I know she's excited she distracted me from the whacked situation with my parents. "Jeremy told me about it before saying anything to David because he wasn't sure how you felt. If you want, I bet he could hook you up. Seriously. Would that not be the *best*?"

"Well, yeah!" I force myself to chill, though. "But don't make me sound desperate or anything. And don't tell Jeremy that

I'm *too* into David, if you haven't already. That'd kill it right off."

"Okay. I didn't say anything to Jeremy, I swear. I wanted to tell you first. "

This is why Christie is number one on my A-list, even if she is Miss Perfect. I guess I'm lucky she's going out with Jeremy, or David would be all over her. They could be Mr. and Miss Perfect.

Oh, damn. What if David's only interested in me because I'm Christie's friend? It wouldn't be the first time a guy asked me out because he thought it'd get Christie to notice him.

Of course, at exactly the moment this occurs to me, a familiar car horn blasts not twenty feet away, practically rendering me deaf.

"Val-er-ieee! Oh, Val-er-ieee!" My mother is pulling into the parking spot nearest to the Dumpster and has her window down. I see Gabrielle in the passenger seat popping the top off a salad and picking out the croutons. Guess they're not whole wheat or something.

I brace myself for Christie to ask who's in the car. Why, why, why me? I hate lying to my friends, and Christie, of all people, would be most likely to understand.

But I am not ready to deal with this. Not yet, not even with Christie. Maybe I can say Gabrielle's a neighbor. No, wait, Christie knows all my neighbors. Maybe someone from the Boosters? Or Mom's book club?

Geez, I despise lying. I don't think I can do it.

My mom sticks her head out the window and asks if we want a ride. Thank goodness, Christie says no, we're heading back to school. My mom waves and takes off, but I can tell she's curious. And so's Christie. Her mouth is hanging open, and she's watching the back of the SUV as it rolls out of the lot.

Book club. I'm going to say Gabrielle's from book club.

"Ohmigod." Christie looks like she's just swallowed her Altoids the wrong way. "What did your mom do to her hair?"

Two

"Dad," I whisper, "what's a timbale?"

I should never have asked him to bring me here. For one, I can't read half the menu. For two, he still hasn't said what decisions we need to make.

And for three, I'm still thinking about David Anderson. And the fact that it's Friday night, which means Jeremy probably won't see him again until Monday at school, since cross-country season is now over and Christmas break is only a week away. No more Saturday meets or practices where they can get together to discuss *moi*.

"It means that it was baked in a mold," Dad explains, and I can tell he's thrilled by his own knowledge of this useless information. I guess it *is* his job. "In most cases, the dish is cream based."

In other words, seafood timbale is probably going to be disgusting. "Oh," I say. "I'm not a fan of creamy."

Or molds. Only Jell-O should go in molds, and even that's iffy. But I don't want to upset Dad, since I did ask to come here and he's shelling out the big bucks.

"Me, either," he says. "But you might like the crab cakes."

I'm not a big seafood person either, but since the rest of the menu's steak (I definitely don't like big hunks of meat), I decide to go with Dad and order the crab cakes to start and the poached snapper. It comes with mushrooms, which I do like.

Honestly, though, I could care less about the food. I want to know what this dinner is all about. It's not just a reward for saving the Mottahedeh from Mom, and we both know it. As soon as the waiter's gone, I look at Dad. I'm just too scared to ask. Thankfully, he brings it up first.

"Valerie, I told you last night we had some decisions to make."

He looks nervous and Martin Winslow rarely gets nervous about speaking. I mean, he's on the speed dial of not only the current president of the United States, but several former presidents, which means he's used to talking to anyone, anytime, about all kinds of strange topics. So I'm tempted to tell him to do whatever, that I don't want to be involved. Especially since my opinions don't seem to carry much weight. I mean, I thought I was being brilliant by suggesting my mom and dad have a cooling-off period before rushing into a divorce. The only way I know my mom even *heard* my opinion was that she later informed me she'd been "cooling off" for a decade.

"Well, now that your mother and I aren't living together any longer, we need to decide where you should live."

Before he's even finished speaking, I can feel tears coming up in my eyes. I try to play it off by taking a long sip of my Diet Coke. I hate that Jules was right about this.

At least she had the Dad-has-a-girlfriend thing wrong.

"Well, I'm not sure Mom wants me

with her," I tell Dad. "Not *living* with her anyway." It's the first time I've said it aloud, but ever since she made her announcement, it's what I've been thinking.

Dad shakes his head, and I start feeling bad for him, too, since Mom definitely doesn't want to live with him. "No," he says, "she does want you to live with her. And so does Gabrielle."

I can tell he hardly wants to let Gabrielle's name pass his lips, but he's making an effort to be polite about it all. He takes a sip of his wine and adds, "I guess she and Gabrielle have a two-bedroom apartment, and you'd have your own bathroom. So it's something to consider."

"But Gabrielle's going to try to tell me what to do, right?" I remember when Jules's stepfather—the guy her mom married in between being married to Jules's dad and remarrying Jules's dad—used to boss her around. One minute he acted like he was her new best buddy, but the next minute—as soon as Jules's mom wasn't around—he'd walk all over her. I remember thinking how glad I was I'd never have to deal with that. But now I guess Gabrielle's going to be my stepmom. Or something.

"I don't know Gabrielle well enough to speak for her," Dad says, his tone making it clear he has no interest in knowing Gabrielle either. "But I know your mom will do her best to make you happy, no matter what problems she and I might have. She loves you as much as she ever has."

I think about this for a minute while I fish a roll out of the bread basket. "Do *you* want me to live with Mom?"

"I want you to do whatever you want. But your mother and I have talked about it, and whatever you decide now, we want you to know you can change your mind. We're not going to fight about custody. We agree that you'll be fine with either of us for the next two and a half years, before you go to college, and that you're mature enough to make your own decision."

Wow. I just stare at Dad. I totally expected him to ask my opinion, just to make me feel like I had a say, then do whatever the hell he and Mom wanted to do.

My dad gives me a look, though, that

clues me in to the fact things aren't so simple.

"What's the catch?"

"Well, if you move in with your mother, you'll switch schools. Her apartment's closer to Lake Braddock. I'm sure you could finish out the year here, but then—"

"Forget it. I hate Lake Braddock." No way do I want to graduate from there. And how could I leave Christie, Jules, and Natalie? Let alone David. Not that I have David to leave—yet. But I never will if I transfer. "Besides, if I stay with you, I can see Mom whenever. I mean, she'll only be a few miles away."

I think this will be okay. I'll have my friends. I won't have to let anyone know what's up with Mom, at least not right away, since I know I'm going to cave and cry if I tell them now. I have to get a grip on this whole thing first.

And Dad won't be so lonely if I'm home. Mom has Gabrielle, but he doesn't have anyone. Well, except me. "I'm staying with you, Dad, definitely." This wasn't nearly as painful as I thought it'd be. "If that's all right, I mean. I kind of like my room, so keeping it would be a plus. And this way I can stay at Vienna West."

Dad twists in his chair, and that's when I notice he hasn't even touched his roll. "That's the other part of the catch, Valerie. But in a way, I think it's good news."

I flip my hand in the air over the table in a get-on-with-it way.

He leans forward and keeps his voice so quiet I can hardly hear him. "I'm about to be transferred."

"Transferred? To where?" As far as I know, there's only one White House, and that's his thing. He's been there since I was five, which means he's on his third president.

"Well, you know President Carew is quite conservative."

"Oh, yeah." He's, like, the hero of the right wing Republicans. The Moral Majority pretty much got him elected. The guy's very progun lobby, antiabortion, and totally against legislation that allows gays to marry or to adopt kids, yadda yadda yadda.

My dad is a registered Democrat, on the other hand. He's voted that way every election since he was eligible. Even though he's occasionally called on to help fix whatever media-catastrophe-of-the-moment there is at the White House, I've never once heard him utter a single word criticizing Republican presidents for their mistakes. Or cheering on the Democrats, come to think of it.

The way I figure, who cares who's in the Oval Office or what they do in their personal lives if the economy is good, health care is improving, and everyone's employed?

But Dad never talks about his political beliefs to anyone. I only know where he stands because I pestered him about it once for a solid week and he finally told me. He also told me it was his job not to have a political opinion, or even a personal opinion of the men he's worked for—some of whom I think drove him insane—so I need to keep the information to myself. Especially the fact he's never voted for a Republican in his life—including the Republicans who've employed him.

"Well, President Carew is up for reelection next year, and his staff will come under a great deal of scrutiny. With your mother and I divorcing, and given the unusual circumstances—"

"You're getting fired because Mom's a lesbian?" I try hard to keep my voice down, but a man at the next table glances our way. I can't help it though. This is just *so* wrong.

"No, Valerie." He reaches across the table and puts his hand over mine, probably as much to shut me up as to comfort me. "No. I felt, with the election coming up, that I needed to tell President Carew what was happening. We both decided it would be best for the administration if I took a job elsewhere. I don't want this to become a political issue any more than he does. Could you imagine if Tim Russert threw it out for discussion on *Meet the Press*?"

I start feeling sick to my stomach, because I know stuff like that happens all the time.

Geez, I hate how D.C. works sometimes.

"The president was very understanding, and he found me another position. A great opportunity, actually." He lets go of my hand, and I can see he's actually excited he's getting canned. "Do you know where Schwerinborg is?"

I do, but only because we did Europe in World History and Geography last year. We had a quiz where we had to fill in all the names of the countries on a map of Europe, and I aced it. Schwerinborg was one of those dinky countries like Andorra, Lichtenstein, and San Marino, where you couldn't write the country name on the actual country. You had to fill it in on a line that pointed to the country.

Most of the class missed it. They either had no clue, or they wrote in "Smorgasbord." We all laughed about that forever, because it totally pissed off the teacher. She thought they were being smart-asses.

"It's very small, and it's in the Alps, between Germany and Switzerland," Dad explains, trying to get me jazzed about this. "They have a lot of skiing, and it's quite beautiful. I'll be chief of protocol to the royal family. I've been offered a two-bedroom apartment in the palace. The palace itself looks a lot like the Louvre—remember when we went there a couple of years ago on vacation?"

I remember the Louvre. I adore art, and spending the afternoon there was the highlight of the trip for me. Warning: The Mona Lisa is underwhelming, but if you ignore that, there's a lot of other good stuff in there. And the building itself is really pretty.

The waiter brings our crab cakes, and they're surprisingly good. "So, let me get this straight," I say between bites. "You're not even going to live in Virginia anymore? You're moving to *Schwerinborg*? And you'll be living in the palace?"

"Yes. Of course, I plan to come back after the next election. Either this president will be out of the White House and a Democrat will be in, so the circumstances of the divorce won't be an issue, or President Carew will bring me back. I have his word, and he isn't a man to go back on his promises." My dad gets a self-satisfied smile on his face. "I'm very good at what I do. Whoever's in the White House will want me there."

"I know."

"But in the meantime, I'd love to have you with me in Schwerinborg. I think it would be a real adventure to get to see more of Europe before you go to college."

"Not that I'm saying yes, because I'm

not . . . but where would I go to school? What's involved here?" I mean, is there a Schwerinborg High? Do I have to learn German? That I *cannot* do. French is my thing. I've had straight A's in it since seventh grade. I think I might even get the French award this year, and that would rock on my college applications since those awards usually go to seniors and the occasional junior, and I'm only a sophomore.

"There's a private American high school near the palace. Prince Manfred and Princess Claudia send their son there to help improve his English. Most of the foreign diplomats' kids attend, as well. The program is impressive. The teachers are primarily Americans, and classes are conducted in English."

My crab cake isn't tasting so good anymore. Going to school at Lake Braddock versus attending some high school with a bunch of foreigners who'll be able to talk about me in German behind my back?

"I'm not getting much of a choice here," I point out, as if this isn't obvious to him. "Either way, I don't get to stay at my school. That's totally unfair."

"I'm sorry, but it's the best I can do. If you decide on Lake Braddock, you'll still see your friends after school."

"No, I won't. None of us have cars." Driver's ed isn't until next semester, and I'm one of the last of my friends to turn sixteen.

"I think your mother will make the effort."

Now I really think I'm going to cry. There's no way I can avoid telling everyone about Mom if I live with her. I mean, what do I say about Gabrielle if she comes to pick me up at school? I lucked out that Christie didn't catch on this afternoon. Jules and Natalie would have immediately, and I can't handle their oh-poor-you-but-I'm-so-glad-it's-not-me sympathy right now.

As much as I love Mom, I really, really don't want to live with Gabrielle. I just know she's going to boss me around and make me eat organic greens and quinoa all the time. Besides, it would just feel weird. How would I handle being around Mom with anyone besides Dad, let alone a new *girlfriend*? I'm as laid back as the next person, but I get uncomfortable around Christie and Jeremy when they start playing tonsil hockey near me.

Then it occurs to me that David Anderson's dad is a big deal conservative lobbyist. David idolizes the man, partially because he was a big college track star, partially because he's always on the *Today* show yammering away about family values with Katie Couric and Matt Lauer. If the president is willing to ship Dad off to Schwerinborg over all this, what's David going to think about me when he hears?

I bet kids who go to high school in Nebraska or California or Minnesota and other *normal* places don't have to deal with this kind of political stuff messing up their relationships.

I swipe a tear off my cheek, because I do *not* want my dad to see me cry. I am not one of those wussy girly-girls who cries to get things my way. Girls like that piss me off.

"Hey, it's going to be okay." I can hear the guilt in Dad's voice, and it makes me feel even worse. "I'll come visit you as often as I can. And if you want, you can come to Schwerinborg during spring break. I have more than enough frequent flyer miles to cover the ticket. We'll go skiing together. Maybe we can go to Interlaken—"

"No, Dad," I interrupt. I'm finally realizing that I'm never, ever going to date David. Because as ticked as I am at my mother right now for ruining my life, I love her, and I can't be someone I'm not just to go out with David Anderson. If he's even interested in me. I mean, come on. One conversation with Jeremy about who I might be dating could mean anything. Right?

"No, what?" A serious pair of wrinkles forms in the space between his eyes as he looks at me. "You wouldn't even visit?"

"No, as in I'm coming with you. I'll move to Schwerinborg. Why the hell not?"

"Don't say hell, Valerie," comes his automatic response. Then he tilts his head at me, and I can tell he's trying very hard not to smile. "Really, though? That's what you want?"

"Yep." I grin, even though I don't really feel like smiling. "That's what I want."

Maybe I'll get lucky and someone there will be as godlike as David. And they won't care how my mom lives her life.

"I don't get it. Why not just suck it up and go to Lake Braddock?" Natalie hisses on Monday morning as our history teacher, Mrs. Bennett, turns her back to start a video on the battles of Gettysburg and Manassas. We've been doing the Civil War in United States and Virginia History for the last three weeks, and frankly, I'm sick of all the blood and gore. At least it'll be over after tomorrow.

On the downside, this Friday is the end of our second quarter, aka major exam time, and the next day I'm off to Schwerinborg. Just like that. Dad says it'll be easiest for me to switch schools between quarters, even though I thought I'd have a *little* more time. Like at least until after Christmas.

This is the one thing I hate about going to Vienna West. We finish each quarter before every other school in the district because our school's used for summer camps and they need us to be out of here earlier in the spring. If we were a normal school, we'd finish second quarter in January and I'd have another month to figure things out. But I don't. Which is what has Natalie so ticked off today.

Ticked off at me, that is. Not the Civil War or our exam schedule.

I ignore Natalie's question, but as soon as the video starts and the room gets dead quiet, a wadded piece of paper comes flying from my right and goes skittering over my desk. I catch it as it goes off the other side, barely keeping it from landing by David Anderson's feet, since he sits in the row next to mine, one seat back. Natalie is a terrible note passer.

I glance at Mrs. Bennett to see if she's noticed, since of course everyone else in the room has, and a few people start snickering. Luckily Mrs. Bennett is focused on grading our quizzes from Friday, and is looking down at her desk, punching numbers on her calculator. Good thing, because if Natalie gets caught with a note in class, especially when she's already grounded, her parents are going to hit the roof.

I frown at Natalie, since I've warned her to lay off the note passing unless it's urgent, then slowly open up the paper, trying to keep the crinkling to a minimum.

Did you at least argue? Ask your mom to maybe get an apartment here in Vienna instead?

Lake Braddock might suck, but it's got to be better than Smorgasbord. I would NEVER move there, just because my parents said so!

ESPECIALLY if David Anderson liked me. What kind of crack are you SMOKING?!?!

I fold up the note and stuff it in my pocket, fast. Natalie glares at me, but no way do I want to get caught with this. Not with David right across the aisle from me. With my luck Mrs. Bennett will catch us and read it out loud to the class. She's done it before.

I take a new sheet of paper from my notebook, uncap a pen, and scribble.

Like you would NEVER stay in Girl Scouts, just because your parents said so?

I know this is a low blow, so below that I add,

(You know what I mean.) I tried, no luck. It won't be so bad, except for missing you guys like crazy. I get to live in a palace and go skiing. And Dad says it won't be long. I'll probably be back for the second half of junior year. That's only a year away.

I know a year is a wicked long time. But since that's two months after elections, and Dad said he'd be able to come back to the White House by then, I figure this is a safe bet. I fold the note—a lot more carefully than Natalie did—and when I'm sure Mrs. Bennett isn't looking, I slide it across the aisle with my foot.

A few minutes later, right when a Confederate cannon goes kerblam and half the class jolts awake, the paper comes flying back onto my desk, hitting me in the hand while I'm taking notes. I almost scream. I'm going to have to talk to Natalie about throwing notes across the aisle during the scary parts.

But what about HIM?!

Him meaning David Anderson, and not Dad, I assume. I look over at Natalie and mouth, "Later!"

She flattens her hands against her cheeks and makes an Edvard Munch–like scream face at me, but I glare at her until she turns back to the video and starts taking notes, since all this stuff will be on the exam, and we only have a few days to go.

I start writing too, but I cannot wrap my brain around the logistics of Pickett's Charge or remember whether General Longstreet was on the Union or Confederate side. Not with Natalie, Jules, and especially Christie so upset. They all cried when I finally told them last night, over Spicy Chicken Fillet Sandwiches and Frostys from the freshly cleaned machine at Wendy's—once Natalie's parents finally agreed she could come out for an hour.

It's nice to know that my buds will miss me, but I feel guilty, too. They think I'm dissing them, and just don't get why I'd move to Schwerinborg, even if staying means I have to go to Lake Braddock and I'd hardly ever see them.

And of course, I can't tell them the whole truth. They don't buy my story about Dad being lonely and me wanting to keep him company either. I think it's because they all secretly believe Jules's girlfriend theory. Like a girlfriend would follow him to Schwerinborg. *Not.* I wouldn't go if the situation here was even remotely tolerable, and I'm his *daughter.* And he's bribing me with ski passes and stuff too.

I can tell that in their minds I'm going to be gone forever, even though I told them over and over that I am so not going to live in freakin' Schwerinborg the rest of my life. I bet they're still getting first-run *Buffy* episodes over there. And although I wouldn't mind seeing the whole Spike/Buffy pseudoromance storyline from the beginning, I'd much rather be in Virginia with all my friends, chilling out in Christie's basement watching MTV *Cribs* or making fun of the idiots who go on *Survivor* and *American Idol.*

I let out a little sigh, then realize it was loud enough for Mrs. Bennett to hear. She's glaring at me, so I yank myself into something resembling good posture and begin watching the video for real.

They keep showing maps of the battle-field, and reenactments of young soldiers running across fields and up hills, fighting for their lives. There's a voiceover, reading letters sent back home by the soldiers. Apparently, as the men were listening to the cannons and guns firing around them, and the agonized cries of their dying friends (which sound totally fake on the video), they weren't thinking about politics or slavery or any of that stuff. They were thinking of home and the mothers and wives and girlfriends they left behind.

I wonder if David will think of me when I'm gone.

I glance over my shoulder. David's totally focused on the video, which doesn't surprise me, because he's got the highest grade in the whole class. Well, except for me, though if I keep allowing the whole Schwerinborg situation to distract me, he may beat me on the exam.

But even just sitting there, staring at the video with the overhead lights off, the guy is totally hot. He's got one elbow on the desk, his fingers forked through his hair, propping up his head. He's taking notes with his other hand, and for a moment, I wonder what it'd be like to sit in the dark and have his fingers interlaced with mine. He has such long, strong fingers.

Is it possible for a guy to have sexy hands?

I'm guessing he's heard my Schwerinborg news. He must have. Christie would have called Jeremy on her cell after we left Wendy's last night, since she was upset and she always cries to Jeremy when she's upset, and Jules told me that David and Jeremy sit together in English during first period.

I start to turn back around so I can figure out the whys and wherefores of Pickett's Charge, but then my eyes catch David's, and I realize he's been watching me stare at him.

Oh, *crap*.

I shift in my chair as subtly as possible, making like I was looking out the window at the quad, where the band geeks are all lined up to practice marching, but we both know I wasn't.

Then he gives me this long, slow wink.

Oh. My. God.

Three

In a panic, I turn back to the video.

Oh. My. God. Ohmigod. I am so busted. What the hell did that *wink* mean?

That I'm a total idiot and he knows it? Or that he's interested?

No. No way, no how, no matter what Christie says. I haven't had a boyfriend since seventh grade, when Jason Barrows kissed me on a dare and everyone went around afterward saying we were boyfriend and girlfriend, which doesn't really count as having a boyfriend, since he wasn't. My boyfriend, that is. Even though everyone told me he had a thing for me because I'm a redhead. I mean, ick.

The bell rings, and Mrs. Bennett gets up to stop the video while everyone rushes to grab their stuff and get out of class before she can give us a new assignment. It's not as if we don't have enough to worry about with exams starting Wednesday. When I lean over to grab my backpack, I see that David is *still* looking at me.

Natalie grabs my arm. "We have got to talk. Now."

But as Natalie yanks me out the door, David shoots me this wicked grin that says, *I know exactly who you're going to talk about too.*

I bet he saw the note Natalie passed me. Bet he read it over my shoulder. Even if Gabrielle's presence wasn't forcing me to already, now I *have* to go to Schwerinborg.

"Wait a minute," I tell Natalie as soon as we're out in the hall. "I think I left my notebook."

I elbow my way back inside as the last few people rush out the door, only to see that Mrs. Bennett has my notebook in her hand. Great.

"Forget this?"

I nod and take it, and she makes some comment about how I can't afford to lose it seeing as I need to ace the next exam if I want to turn my A into an A+ for the term. Then she blows by me on her way to the teachers' lounge, since this is her break period.

She must've seen Natalie pass that note, or at least she suspects. Otherwise she'd never be on my back about my grade. I mean, really. I bet *she* didn't have as high a grade when she was a sophomore. Sometimes you just know you've got more book smarts than one of your teachers.

I drop my backpack on top of the nearest desk and unzip it to shove my notebook inside while I try to figure out what to say to Natalie. I so don't want to argue about this with her anymore, but I just know she's going to be all over me about moving once I go back into the hall.

"Hey, Val."

I look up, and there's David. Like, RIGHT there. Either he never left the room, or he followed me back in. How could I not have seen him? Usually I can tell whenever he's within a hundred-yard radius. After all these years of having an insane crush on him, I've developed a finely tuned David radar.

"Um, hey." This is about all I can manage, which makes me sound like a total dork. I mean, we've known each other forever, and we're kind of friends, so what's my problem? "What's up?"

He sits on top of the desk next to my backpack. I think I'm going to keel over, right here in room 104. David's butt is actually touching my backpack. Since I'm busy trying to unstick the zipper, I can't help but see the fabulous way his Levi's curve around his rear. And if I pull the backpack zipper all the way around, I could touch him. If I wanted.

Once last month I saw Christie and Jeremy waiting for a ride after Christie finished volleyball practice, and she had her arms around his waist, with her index fingers hooked in the back pockets of his jeans while he kissed her. At the time I thought it was kind of weird, but now I'm thinking I'd like to have my fingers hooked in David's pockets. Oh, yeah. I can definitely see how that would be fun.

He scoots on the desk, and I realize I'm staring at him. Again. I make myself focus on his eyes and try not to turn red. Of course, since I'm about as fair skinned as a human being can be, that's pretty much impossible.

And did I mention that his eyes are phenomenal?

"I, uh, I heard you're moving to, um . . ."

"To Schwerinborg."

He smiles, but only on one side of his mouth. Could he be any more delicious? "Yeah. Of all places. Can't believe you're going to Smorgasbord. Who'da thought?"

I need a ventilator. Not only has David heard my news, he wants to *talk* about it?

"I'll miss you, Winslow. I know we don't hang out as much as when we were kids or anything, but I've always thought you're one of the few truly cool people in this place. Plus, you're the only person who can outscore me in history. What'll I do without you here to challenge me?"

My mouth can't form a reply, since I'm thinking, *Me, cool?* Me, with my whacked red hair and freak show green eyes, when he is a complete and total sex god who can go out with anyone in the entire universe? Or at least with anyone in the entire school—which is still a hell of a lot of people, seeing as there are twenty-five hundred students at West Vienna High.

He stands up, and his gorgeous butt is no longer in contact with my backpack. "Will you have e-mail there?"

"I think so."

He fishes a piece of paper out of his notebook and scribbles down his e-addy. "In case I forget later, with exams and all. Let me know what's up with you over there, okay?"

"Yeah, I will."

As I slide the piece of paper into my jeans pocket, he says, "I'd really like to keep in touch. I've been thinking lately that we should hang out more. It'd still be cool to chat, even if it's long distance now."

"That'd be cool." Cool. Understatement of the year.

He smiles back, then he leans over and gives me a lightning-quick kiss on the cheek before walking out the door.

I cannot move.

A few seconds later Natalie comes back in, but I don't even see her. I hear her first.

"Come *on,* Valerie. What is with you?"

David. David is what's with me. Oh, *crap.*

Given the way this afternoon deteriorated on its way to evening, I should be really, really fried right now.

It's seven P.M., and my dad *just* got home from work, which means I had to settle for chewy reheated pizza, even though he promised me yesterday he'd get home in time to make his divinely inspired chicken marsala. Why scientists can't come up with microwave technology that makes a zapped pizza taste as good as one right out of the oven is beyond me, but that's actually not the main reason I should be upset right now.

I glance across the kitchen toward Dad, who's tuned in to CNN and shaking his head at some berserker pundit who's ranting about the Democrats (of course) and how if they'd just been a little nicer to the Republicans, and supported them and their last proposed tax cut and a million other issues, maybe people would have voted differently in the last election and President Carew wouldn't be in the White House. According to this freak, Democrats like my mom (and secretly, my dad) aren't nice people, and that's why they aren't in the White House.

I hate listening to this stuff, because a) I really don't care about politics unless they directly affect me, which is practically never; and b) I know it's upsetting to Dad, who tries so hard to like everybody and be tolerant and play fair. That's how he manages to keep his job no matter who's in office.

And the icing on tonight's cake? My mother—the main reason Dad has to leave the job he loves—is on her way over. She's going to be taking care of the house while we're in Schwerinborg, and Dad has a few things he wants to go over with her. I just know they're going to get into it. Okay, not flinging dishes or anything, like divorcing couples always seem to on those Lifetime made-for-television movies, but still.

I'm not *really* upset by any of this,

though. Really. Pizza, loudmouthed politicians, even Mom can't faze me tonight.

I mean, David Anderson KISSED ME.

Not a genuine, pressed-up-against-my-locker-between-classes-clawing-each-other's-clothes kiss, the way I've always dreamed he'd kiss me. But it was definitely premeditated—I mean, he was *waiting* for me to come get my notebook, or at least watching for an opportunity to get me alone—which makes me think maybe Christie was right. Maybe he really does like me.

After all these years of secret lust, scribbling *Valerie Anderson* and *Valerie Winslow Anderson* and the totally un-PC *Mrs. David Anderson* in the blank pages of my diary (because who has time to actually write real stuff in a diary?) before shredding the pages into the trash, mortified with my juvenile behavior—is it possible he feels the same way?

The sound of my dad snorting at the television brings me back to the real world. This man is taking me to Schwerinborg in five days. If I go, I might never find out what David's really thinking. What am I going to DO?!?

Dad did say I could change my mind. So maybe I should. Or not. Oh, damn, damn, and triple damn.

I mean, it isn't like David hasn't had years and years to kiss me before now. Or at least give me his e-addy, if he wanted to talk or get to know me as a better-than-casual friend.

But does any of that matter if he's interested *now*?

Then I realize why Dad is being so uncharacteristically vocal with the television. David's father is on and he's spewing his lobbyist crap.

What an unfortunate little co-inkee-dink.

I scoot to the edge of my chair for a better look. Mr. Anderson's head is neatly framed in a little box that says *Washington* under it. There's also a sharply dressed man in a box marked *Boston* and a prudish woman with square glasses above *San Francisco*. And they're all saying that Carew was elected because people believe in his values, and that he has an excellent chance of being reelected. David's dad loudest of all. Okay. *Now* I'm upset.

I let my head thunk against the table.

This is too much for one day. Why, why, why does David have to think every word out of his dad's mouth is gospel? And why do I have to hear all about Carew's value system via CNN, when those values are now ruining my entire freakin' life?

"Valerie?" Dad clicks off the set. "You all right?"

I lift my head off the table. "Oh, peachy."

Dad raises an eyebrow. "Is it Wolf Blitzer, or the fact your mother's on her way over?"

I try not to laugh. How many problems can I accumulate in one day? On top of the fact that I have a ton of geometry formulas to memorize before this week's exam. Geometry is—thankfully and surprisingly— much easier for me than algebra was last year (algebra was created by Satan, I'm con- vinced), but it's still no cakewalk. I'd rather take ten Friday quizzes from Mrs. Bennett than one end-of-quarter geometry exam.

And we won't even discuss the paper I have due in English on *Billy Budd*. My theory is that if Herman Melville wanted anyone to actually read it, he'd have called it *Killing a Sailor* or *Hang the Dude!* or something equally attention grabbing.

"Look," Dad says, "your mother and I have our problems, but we're working them out. We don't hate each other, and we're not going to fight over furniture or place settings tonight."

Good, I'm thinking, because what's the point in having all the nice furniture if we're going to Schwerinborg, anyway?

"How about we ask her to stay for a movie?" Dad crosses the kitchen and rubs my shoulder. "I'll let you choose. What's that DVD you just bought with the medieval knight?"

"*A Knight's Tale?*"

"Sure. It looks interesting."

"Mom won't like it." She's into the indie film scene—the stuff that plays at Sundance and maybe a couple of art-fart theaters around your major metropolitan areas, if the producers are lucky. Not anything with drool-licious men like Heath Ledger wearing chain mail.

"What we watch isn't the issue," Dad says just as the doorbell rings. "Your mom wants to spend as much time as possible with you before we leave, and watching a movie together would make for a nice evening."

"What about you, though?" I drop my voice to a whisper and follow him to the door. "I mean, if it bugs you being around Mom, I can go watch a movie at her place." Even if it has one of those go-nowhere plots I don't quite get.

"Look, Valerie," Dad doesn't even bother to lower his voice, and I know for a fact you can hear what's said in the front hall from the front porch even when the door is closed. "Go wherever *you're* most comfortable. I've known your mother for nearly twenty years. I'm not happy about the divorce, but she's still the best friend I've ever had. We can handle seeing a movie together."

If it was me whose wife was leaving me for another woman, I'd sure feel uncomfortable having her over for movies and popcorn. Too much like a date, even if your daughter is there and everything is ostensibly "for the sake of the kid." But I guess Dad's a better person than I am.

"Okay," I shrug as he flips the deadbolt on the front door. "Just checking."

This could be fun. I mean, if the two of them are nicey-nice, it might feel like it used to, before Mom upended everything. I could use a dose of that kind of normalcy, even if it's only for tonight and I know it's not for real.

I smile at Mom, but I can tell from her face—as she and Dad walk through the house and discuss which plants need watering, how the alarm system works, and who to call when the sprinkler system needs to be turned on in the spring, since these are always tasks that fell to Dad—that she's still surprised I decided to go to Schwerinborg with Dad instead of staying with her. She keeps glancing at me to see if I'm cool.

When we go into the family room for the movie, I work up the guts to ask Mom where Gabrielle is. If that blond mom stealer is going to show up and plop on the sofa next to me while Heath Ledger is midtournament, I need advance notice.

Mom says Gabrielle's out for the evening though. Get this: at a Weight Watchers meeting.

Shock must be as apparent on my face as

it is on Dad's, because my mother instantly looks from me, to my dad, and back to me before saying, "And what's wrong with that?"

"Nothing wrong with it. Just . . . interesting." Dad hustles to pop the disc into the DVD player just to escape the issue, I'm sure, so Mom turns to me.

"Valerie?"

I can't help but snort out loud. I'm not as polite as Dad. "Interesting 'cause she's built like Brittany Murphy and Calista Flockhart. Total rail. She lives on vegetables and soy and stuff, right?"

"She used to be eighty pounds heavier," Mom explains, using her I-wish-you-would-give-Gabrielle-a-break voice. "She was quite unhealthy. Borderline diabetic even. Her doctor sent her to Weight Watchers, and that prompted her to look into yoga and healthy living, and that's how she became a vegan. Now that she's lost the weight, she's a lifetime member. Going to meetings every so often keeps her focused on living a clean, healthy life. I really admire her for it."

This from the woman who believes

chicken nuggets and SpaghettiOs to be food groups in their own right? What she has with Gabrielle *must* be love.

I don't say anything, so Mom shoots a pointed look toward the kitchen, where the empty pizza box is sitting on the counter. "You could probably learn from her, Valerie. How many times have you eaten fast food in the last week?"

Oh, *please.* I hold up the popcorn I made for the movie. "Microwave light. Can't be that bad."

She ignores me and looks at Dad, who's now sitting in the chair as far from her as possible, remote in hand. "You're going to watch what she eats while you're over there in Europe, aren't you, Martin?"

"Mom!" I mean, it's not like *she's* a vegan or a size four. And if she gets on Dad's case again, I'll remind her of her own little trip to Wendy's last week. Gabrielle might've had a salad, but I saw that Biggie Value Meal bag in Mom's lap.

Thankfully the movie starts, allowing me to enjoy a little eye candy in the form of Heath Ledger. I think I'll pretend he's David. A nonpolitical, totally-into-me David.

"I think David Anderson looks a lot like Heath Ledger."

It's ten thirty and I should be asleep, since tomorrow's a school day, but I can't settle. I have David on the brain. And Jules keeps her cell phone, with the ringer turned on low, on her nightstand, so we can chat in the middle of the night without her parents realizing she's awake either.

"Well, the hair, for sure," Jules says. "But not his eyes. David's are much nicer. More open, and green instead of brown. Heath's are brown, right? And David has a slimmer nose." She giggles, which is disturbing because Jules hardly ever giggles. "I can't *believe* he kissed you—or that you waited until lunch to tell me about it. I told Natalie that now you can't go to Schwerinborg. You can't know how totally stoked I am over this."

"On the cheek," I remind her. "And I'm going. I have to."

Jules gets really quiet, I guess because I told her the other night at Wendy's that I didn't *have* to go, that my parents were totally cool and gave me a choice. So I say, "Come on. Between this thing with David and you guys ragging on me, you're making me feel like shit on a sidewalk. This isn't an easy decision for me." They don't have half a clue how hard it really is.

"But you've loved David forever. And you're leaving *us*," Jules whines. "What the hell is going on with you? Something you're not telling me."

I roll over in bed so I'm facing my wall. I photocopied David's yearbook picture last spring and stuck it to a tiny spot near my head where I can hide it with my bed pillows, so Mom and Dad won't know how totally obsessed I am. And so David's the last guy I see before I go to bed at night. Pathetic. I know.

I use my fingernail to lift the tape at the edge of the photo, and pull it off the wall so David's stamp-sized face is flirting with me from my fingertip. "You've seen *A Knight's Tale*, right, Jules?"

"Yeah."

"Well, at the end of the movie, who's Heath with? The snotty princess. I didn't like her at all. She was totally manipulative and he didn't even see it. He should have gone for the girl who made his armor instead. I mean, she saved his life with that armor, she was able to hang with his friends without dissing them like the princess did, and she was kind of cute. But he hardly even noticed her."

"And this has to do with Schwerinborg how?"

Júles can be annoying when she wants to be. I squash up the photocopied picture and toss it into the trash. "Duh. I'm the Armor Girl."

Jules groans, even though it sounds muffled by her sheets. "Get over it, Winslow. You're so not an Armor Girl."

"Yes, I am. Think. In the movie, Heath doesn't really know the Armor Girl—not the way she is on the inside. He likes having her around, she pushes him to be a better person, but he doesn't really care about knowing her. He's all caught up in the Shallow Princess because she's gorgissimo, despite the fact that her incredibly stupid, completely selfish prove-your-love-to-me-by-losing-the-tournament demands nearly get him killed."

I flip onto my back and stare at the ceiling. "This is what *all* hot guys do, Jules. They take practical Armor Girls for granted, and to the world at large, this is okay. Everyone cheers when hot guy runs off with idiot Shallow Princess at the end, and the movie does a hundred mil at the box office. Armor Girl gets a kiss on the cheek and a scribbled e-mail address."

"That's bull. Besides, how do you know you're not David's princess?"

Hello? How long has Jules known me? I'm not bad looking, but certainly no princess. I'm a passable Armor Girl. And David knows me about as well as Heath knew the Armor Girl.

And even if David *did* get to know me, he'd always be able to ditch me for some princess. A Republican princess with a nice C cup, hair blonder than his, and a cute smile like Reese Witherspoon's. Certainly someone whose mother didn't have a midlife crisis involving a trip out of the proverbial closet.

"Well, let's see. I'm not a cheerleader, and I goof on those who are. I don't have naturally bouncy hair and don't buy every single article of clothing from Bebe. And I would *never* tell a guy to lose a game to prove he's in love with me."

"But that doesn't mean—"

"Look, Jules, I'm dying that he kissed me. But I have to be honest with myself here. He's had his chances. And he's dated Shallow Princesses for as long as I can remember."

"Well, I think it's wrong that you're not giving him another chance. You're as bad as the Shallow Princess in the movie, you just can't see it. You're moving to Schwerinborg to test his love."

"Yeah, sure. And my parents agreed to get divorced just so I could test my theory."

She's quiet. I can tell she's mad, but I can't figure out why. I mean, it's not her who's the loser Armor Girl in this scenario. And I feel like I'm having a moment of great personal growth here— being able to have David kiss me and still walk away, knowing it's the best thing. Maybe this means there's someone better out there for me. Maybe even in Schwerinborg.

Someone who'd consider me a not-shallow princess.

You'd think Jules would see that.

"Look," Jules finally says. "I don't think you should make major life decisions based on Heath Ledger movies."

"The decision's already made. I was just using the movie to illustrate the point so you, Christie, and Natalie would understand."

"Well, if you want to analyze your life in terms of a Heath Ledger movie, try *The Four Feathers*. Especially the beginning."

I hear my dad coming down the hall, so I tell her I'll check it out, since I haven't seen that one yet, and that I'll see her tomorrow, but not to be mad.

After my dad sticks his head in my door to make sure I'm asleep, and I'm alone again in the dark and quiet, I decide I should be thankful Jules didn't nail me with *10 Things I Hate About You*. Then the movie trailer for *The Four Feathers* comes back to me. Duh. Thanks, Jules.

The Four Feathers is the one where all Heath's friends accuse him of betrayal for not sticking with the group when things get rough, and not even bothering to give them a good explanation.

Which, in a way, is even worse than *10 Things I Hate About You*. It's group hate.

Four

I thought, for a brief three weeks, that my mother ruined my life. I was sadly, sadly mistaken. I have done it quite by myself.

Northern Virginia is sunny and filled with places to hang out. Parks. Malls. Even fast-food joints like Jules's Wendy's, though clearly that's just where losers like me tend to congregate.

Schwerinborg, on the other hand, is prison gray. Everywhere. The sky, the apartment buildings and cathedrals, even the mountains are gray. Okay, I assume that it's mostly gray because it's December and foggy. But still. I'm not seeing teenagers. *Anywhere.*

"Valerie," my dad whispers. He doesn't have to elaborate. His warning tone, combined with a disturbing divot forming between his eyes, is enough.

I yank my fingers out of my mouth, but reluctantly. I can't help it—whatever that bizarre party mix was they gave us on the Lufthansa flight from Munich to Freital, the capital (and frankly, I think the only real city) of Schwerinborg, is now permanently lodged between my gum and molar, and it hurts. But I suppose trying to pick it out while seated next to my dad, in a *limo*, no less, is a major faux pas.

Wonder what the German term is for *faux pas*?

Folkschen paschken?

This whole German thing has me in knots. In the Munich airport, where we switched planes, all the signs were in English, French, and German.

Here, it's all German, all the time. I can't figure out a thing, although *ausfahrt* is apparently the word for "exit," since I see it on every ramp.

I probably shouldn't think too hard about that one, or I'll be grossed out. Don't want to spew chunks in the back of the limo, which was pretty nifty of Prince Manfred, my dad's new boss and the ruler of this dinky little country, to send to pick us up. Definitely a step above working for President Carew. When he sent a car for my dad, it was only a Buick.

Though I'm still wondering if, while this is great for Dad, I've screwed myself royally by coming here. At least they speak English at Lake Braddock. Plus Jules and Natalie stopped speaking to me—in any language—from Tuesday to Friday, though they did show up at the house on Saturday, a couple hours before Dad and I left for the airport, so they could say good-bye.

They didn't apologize for ignoring me all week though. Even if they are pissed off, that's no excuse. I mean, we've been friends for *years*. You'd think they'd want to spend as much time as possible together during my last few days, but no.

Christie was better, but not much. She kept talking to me all week at least, but never in front of Jules or Natalie, and she kept giving me these weepy looks that made me want to smack her beautiful, unblemished face. I understood though. Jules and Natalie were going hard core on her, trying to get her to pressure me into staying. I'd probably have caved to the Jules-Natalie assault machine if I'd been in Christie's shoes.

I almost caved myself, right before Dad and I left for the airport, when it was just me and Christie alone in my room for the last time. We were talking about all the stuff I'm going to miss next semester—like track season, driver's ed, and the art class trip up to New York to tour the museums—and I started to get emotional. Then Christie asked me where Mom was, and how come she wasn't there to say good-bye.

I used the book club excuse I'd concocted at Wendy's, but I came just-this-close to telling Christie everything. Only the thought that Christie would probably tell Jeremy (and therefore, through the grapevine, David, Jules, and Natalie) the real scoop about my parents' divorce forced me to zip my lip.

The limo takes a sharp turn, past one of the signs saying *ausfahrt*, of course. At the top of the ramp, we turn twice more, then head into a downtown area. The streets are much, much narrower than in D.C., and most of them are made of cobblestone, which is pretty neat. We pass through a congested square with a statue in the center, and I'm trying to figure out who's riding the sculpted horse (I'm guessing it's not Napoleon), when atop a slight hill, I see a true *edifice.* I love that word but never get to use it. This place justifies it.

I grab my dad's arm and ask if it's the palace. I get to see a lot of awesome buildings, living near D.C., but this rocks them all.

"It is." Dad's happy I'm excited about something for the first time in at least a week. "Think you can stand living there?"

I squint up as the limo driver pulls onto a side road and noses the car uphill, toward the building. Now that we're closer, I can see that it's definitely Louvre-like. It's constructed of gray stone, and looks a bit like D.C.'s nicer office buildings, but with columns and detailed trim under the eaves. The windows are all beyond tall, and hung with what I'm guessing are very expensive curtains. There are carvings of goddesses on the exterior, in between each of the windows.

No kidding. *Goddesses.*

I cannot imagine *living* in a place like this.

"If the inside's as pretty as the outside, I think I'll make do," I tell Dad. As long as I don't drop a Diet Coke on a fancy silk chair or one of the antique rugs or anything. And so much for eating sushi, if they even have it in Schwerinborg. I tend to spray soy sauce everywhere when I eat. You'd think Dad would be able to teach me the trick to that though.

I'm just about to ask him, but thank God, we pass a McDonald's, and it's walking distance from the palace! Happy, happy, joy, joy. At least if I need a fry fix, I'm covered.

Four hours later, after getting a tour of the palace, filling out paperwork, and making a two-minute exploration of our apartment—and two minutes is all it needs, since apparently a palace "apartment" is pretty much like a hotel suite, meaning a couple of rooms off a second-floor hallway—Dad is kind enough to give me the McChicken I've been craving. Between sips of Diet Coke—excuse me, Coke *Light*—I gently point out that, contrary to exterior appearances, our new place isn't exactly the Ritz.

The furnishings in our apartment are somewhat . . . spare. Not spare in a Calvin Klein, black-and-gray, ultramodern way, but spare as in basic. In sharp contrast to the heavy tapestries and floor-to-ceiling mirrors that are in the main hallways and public areas of the palace, our apartment boasts two sofas worthy of a Holiday Inn. Across from the sofas, there's a TV—with cable, thankfully—set on top of a rickety black melamine stand.

Dad's room has a double bed, a dresser, and a small bathroom. My bedroom, on the opposite side of what I'll call the living room, is painted an uninspired brown. I have to wonder who decorated the place. I mean, who sleeps in a brown room? It has a twin bed, an armoire that my dad calls a *schrunk,* and a minuscule bathroom. The shower is beyond small, so I have no clue how I'm going to shave my legs. And there's not even a countertop where I can put my stuff. Just a pedestal sink.

I do not want to keep my face wash on the back of the toilet. I mean, *really*. I tell Dad that *schrunk* should be the German word for "bathroom," not for "armoire," because honestly, the armoire thingie is about the same size as the bathroom.

What's worse, the electrical outlets are all weird, and Dad says I'm going to have to buy a new hair dryer, since mine won't work here. I forgot about that from our trip to France last year. I hadn't bothered to do my hair then, since I knew I wouldn't meet any cute French guys with my parents two inches off my elbow the entire time.

Unfortunately we can't go shopping for a couple days, because Dad says he has to acquaint himself with his new job and his new boss. Bummer, because that means I won't be able to commence my David Anderson look-alike hunt anytime soon. It's pretty much the only thing I have to do in this country until school starts, so I figure I should take the time to make sure my hair isn't completely ugly.

And that's the whole apartment, other than the eat-in kitchen—complete with a Formica-topped table and four terribly tacky chairs—where I'm rapidly discovering that Schwerinborg's version of a McChicken comes with a sauce that smells vaguely of onions.

At least the fries are good. Dad scored some ketchup to go with them, which is a relief. We had trouble with that in France—they eat 'em with mayo, for some bizarre reason. But the French can be excused their quirks because they speak such a kickin' language.

"Valerie? Thanks." Dad sets down his Big 'N Tasty and gives me a smile like I haven't seen on him in a long, long time.

"For what?"

"For coming. I know this isn't like home, and the adjustment isn't going to be easy, but having you here with me means more than you'll ever know."

I take another bite of my McChicken. I'm actually having fun sitting here with Dad, just the two of us, but I don't want to *talk* about it. I get uncomfortable when Dad gets all mushy on me, because he never used to. It's like an alien infiltrated his brain the day Mom decided to go gay. Or, I should say, *the day she made her emotional breakthrough and realized her true self.*

Someday I really will be able to think about my mom in PC terms. And when I do, I'll mean it. Just not today.

"You know, Valerie, change is hard on everyone. Even an old geezer like me," he jokes. He's older, yeah, but no geezer, and he knows it. I saw at least three different women checking him out during our tour of the palace this afternoon. "This experience is what we make it, though. I think this could turn out to be a wonderful thing for both of us."

"Just as long as you take me skiing. Soon," I tease him. He's *got* to lighten up. "When does school start here, anyway? They're out for Christmas now, right?"

"They finished their second quarter same day you did. You don't start—officially—for two weeks. But I'm afraid there are some placement exams you'll need to take. Just so you're in the right classes."

I drop my McChicken back onto its wrapper. "Hey. You didn't tell me that!"

"It's not a big deal, Valerie. The exams aren't the be-all and end-all of your placement. The school will also be looking at your transcripts and talking to you about which textbooks you were using and how much material your teachers in Virginia covered. And I know your school guidance counselor wrote up a report on how well you were doing in all your classes."

I steal a couple of his fries. I figure he owes me, since any exam is a big deal, as far as I'm concerned. "When do I take these?"

"You'll take two this week, and two next. So if we go skiing, it'll just be a quick day trip. I think it's wise for you to be well rested. Don't you?"

He grabs some of my fries, just to get back at me. I find it hysterical he does this with me, since he's so hoity-toity in public. I'm just waiting for the day he forgets who he's with and mooches off the First Lady's plate.

He pops a fry into his mouth and says, "You're not going to bail on me because of a few exams, are you?"

"No, not yet," I tell him, though he's got to know that I'm only half serious.

"Well, if it helps, I do have another surprise for you."

"Only if it's better than Mickey D's."

'Cause that's about the biggest surprise of my day so far, and on the grand scale of things, getting a meal that's sure to make my butt expand isn't exactly memorable. And it better not be one of those Chicken Soup books that's supposed to cure my messed-up teenage soul. Like some bizarro introvert writer spewing platitudes can fix *my* life. Hah.

"I think so." Dad wads up the burger wrappers and tosses them into the trash can beneath the kitchen sink. "What if I told you that Prince Manfred has arranged to have a computer, complete with cable Internet access, set up for us in about an hour?"

"Really? Then I say, 'Bring it on, Manny!'" Contact with the outside world? Wha-hoo!

"Valerie—" My dad's warned me for days that I have to be on my "public" behavior at all times at the palace.

"Oh, *come on*. You know I won't refer to him that way to anyone but you. I'm not a complete idiot." Good thing I'm an only child. I think I'm pretty normal, but if my dad had another kid to compare me to, especially one with his meticulous personality, I'd be in trouble.

"Just to be sure, you won't be here when the tech guys arrive."

"You're sending me *out*? Alone?" That's what he thinks.

"Just to the library. There's a small one here in the palace, and it's very easy to find. I have a list of what's covered on each of the placement exams, and Prince Manfred was kind enough to have your teachers send over copies of the textbooks you'll be using." Dad opens up one of the cabinets built into the wall of our living room and yanks out a stack of books. Same geometry text I had in Vienna, I notice. Same French book too. The rest are totally unfamiliar, but at least they're in English.

Dad sets them on the table in front of me, then drops the list on top. "Take an hour or two to look it all over tonight, and you'll be set."

I am not believing this. I just got off what has to be the longest plane flight ever, and he wants me to cram? I cross my arms over my chest. "I thought you said I wouldn't have to study."

"It's not as bad as it looks. You just finished studying for your second-quarter exams last week, so you should be in good shape. Now quit making faces and remember that it's not going to be graded. It's just to get a general idea of what you've been exposed to."

"Dad—"

"When you get back, the computer will be ready. And I'll see if I can get the fridge stocked in the meantime. All right?"

He can always bribe me with food. It's pathetic. You'd think after my McChicken, this wouldn't work. But it does. *Stock the fridge* in Martin Winslow language generally means he's going to have something tasty for me while I veg out on the couch later.

I grab the list and look it over. Most of it isn't too bad, but I'm going to have to remind myself how to diagram a sentence. We did that last year and I promptly forgot how. The way I figure, I can *write* a competent sentence, so why the hell would I need to diagram one? I bet Shakespeare never diagrammed a sentence, and he turned out just fine.

Dad gives me directions to the library, puts the textbooks, a blank notebook (like I'm supposed to take notes? As if!), and a pencil in my hands, then shoves me out the door.

Thankfully, the library's not as gray and boring as everything else. There's a lot of light from the windows, which overlook the whole city, and the oriental rugs are all a bright, cheery red. And unlike our apartment (which you'd think would be nicer, being in a palace and all), there's not a square inch of Formica to be seen. Just some comfy-plus armchairs, two long tables I'm certain are antiques, a fireplace, and walls and walls of books. Old, expensive-looking books on polished, dark shelves.

I think I'm in heaven. I love libraries, and this has to be one of the best on the cozy scale.

I settle down in the chair closest to the fireplace, since someone on the staff—which I'm discovering is huge and mostly invisible—has built a fire and left a neatly stacked pile of logs to the side of the marble hearth. Of course, this means I spend a full fifteen minutes staring at the fire and not opening the geometry book.

I finally give up and open my notebook, figuring that if I scribble out a few formulas, Dad will feel like he's being a good parent and I'm being a good kid. But instead of writing anything geometry related, I start sketching.

I have no idea what I want to do careerwise, though I can guarantee it won't involve algebra or geometry. But if newsrooms are still using artists to sketch court scenes ten years from now—you know, those penciled pictures they flash on Court TV or MSNBC when there aren't any cameras allowed in the courtroom—I'd love to do that for a living. I started back in sixth or seventh grade by sketching my teachers when I got bored in class. I'm awesome at faces and at showing emotions, and I draw fast. Obviously, I'm bored a lot.

Within a few minutes, I have a killer drawing. It's me, Jules, Natalie, and Christie. Just our faces, all in a row, grinning at each other. I'm just about to pencil in David's face when a voice behind me scares the bejesus out of me.

And I don't understand a freaking word other than *Valerie.*

"I'm sorry," I mumble once I've righted myself in the chair. I tend to sit sideways in armchairs, which gives Dad a near stroke when we're in public. *"Sprechen Sie Englisch?"*

This is the only sentence I know in German. Yes, it's pitiful.

Even worse than my attempt at German, I think I am going to have a stroke myself, right here in the palace library, now that I can see the guy. He's standing about five feet behind me, near one of the long library tables. The face attached to the German-speaking voice is mesmerizing. Not necessarily handsome—well, at least not in a David Anderson look-alike way—but he's definitely not bad. And he's *my age.*

"I apologize." He sticks out his hand, and it's even sexier than David's. Be still my heart! "I forgot you don't speak German. I'm Georg."

He says it like "GAY-org." Not the world's most attractive name. Not by a long shot. And the less I have to hear about anything gay right now, the better. Yes, I'm just that shallow. But his accent is one hundred percent to die for. I can ignore the name to hear that accent again. Yum.

And suddenly I get self-conscious about the fact I'm in my Adidas track pants and a T-shirt, with my hair in a ponytail.

I shake his hand and smile. "I'm Valerie Winslow. But it sounds like you already knew that."

"I hope you don't mind my intrusion. I saw you sitting in here, and thought I'd introduce myself."

"It's no intrusion," I say. Like I wanted to be sitting here studying geometry? But I can't say that, because this guy sounds almost as formal and polite as my dad. I've never met a teenager as stiff as this dude.

"My father told me you were moving in." He leans forward, putting his elbows on the back of the armchair next to mine. "It'll be nice to have another high schooler around here. I hate being the only nonadult in this place."

"You live here?" I hadn't thought about it, but I guess if my dad and I get an apartment here, it only makes sense that some of the other staff get them too. "Do your parents work here?"

"They sure do." A slow, totally hot smile spreads across his face. I *so* want to draw it. It's just that fascinating and different. Kind of crooked and very Colin Farrell–esque.

It's like I can actually *see* him letting down his guard, and I get that feeling of relief that comes from knowing the other person you're talking to has decided you're cool.

Okay, he's not David Anderson. But he's growing on me. Definitely.

"Cool." I wave for him to sit down. "You like it here?"

He walks around and takes a seat. He doesn't flop like most guys would. Even though he looks completely relaxed—I think it's the whole Colin Farrell thing he has going—he sits properly, without putting his feet on the chair or anything, unlike me. Dad would love this guy. Which also makes me think maybe Dad's right and I'm going to have to spruce up my etiquette skills before anyone else here sees me.

I'm also guessing now that Georg's maybe a year or so older than me. Don't know why—there's just something about him. Confidence, maybe? And his English is fantastic. Better than my French, and I really work hard at it. "I like it well enough, but it's my home country, so I'm biased. What do you think so far?"

I shrug, but not the leave-me-alone-already shrug I give my parents. This one's more polite. "I've only been here since ten A.M. Not much time to get a real impression."

"That's diplomatic. You can be honest."

I know I just met this guy, but his smile gives me the feeling he's for real. I think this about very, very few people, so I decide to tell the truth. "Well, Schwerinborg is pretty gray. And kind of boring. But I'm willing to give it time." I say this in a jokey-jokey voice, 'cause I don't want to offend him or anything. For all I know, he loves living here.

"It's not this gray all the time. I promise." I can tell from the look in his eyes he's trying to gauge my reaction to what he's saying, and I must still be doing all right, because he isn't as formal as when he first walked in and said hello. "It's not going to be like living in the States, though. You're not going to be able to hang out at a mall. Or make fun of the contestants in the Miss Teen USA pageant."

"That's okay. I can't handle pageants, even as a form of amusement, and I'm definitely not the mall type. And if I get really homesick, I can always go to McDonald's."

He grins. "True. I hardly ever get to eat there, but I could nosh on fries all day."

I can't help but laugh. "Did you just say 'nosh'?" It sounds so bizarre, coming out in that accent.

One of his dark eyebrows arches up. "That's not right?"

"It's right. I just wouldn't think it'd be a word you'd use. Your English is amazing."

"I've had to take it since kindergarten. If it's no good now, I'm in trouble." He gestures toward my notebook. "But I could never draw like that. No matter how many classes I had."

Oh, geez. I still have my sketch on my lap. I'm always careful in class not to let anyone see what I'm doing. Not so much because my teachers will get their panties in a twist about it, but because I don't want my friends telling me I made them look fat or made their lips too big or whatever.

"It's no big deal, really. I'm supposed to be studying—"

"You're very talented." He shifts a little closer on his chair and leans forward for a better look. "Are those your friends?"

I nod. I'd shut my notebook, but that seems like it'd be rude at this point.

"Do you draw all your friends?"

"I suppose so. Not intentionally, or anything. My pencil just starts going with whatever's on my mind. So at some point, all my friends and family get sketched."

"I bet they're flattered."

I shake my head. "Are you kidding? They think I make them look awful."

He runs a finger across the top of my notebook, just above Natalie's head, then taps the paper. "If that's awful, then your friends must all look like supermodels. If you ever drew me, I certainly wouldn't complain. I'm sure you'd do a great job."

Is Georg flirting with me? Whoa. Guys do *not* flirt with me. Especially not guys with accents. I mean, that David kiss last week is about the only flirting I've had in my whole freakin' *life.* And it took me *years* to get to that point with David.

"Are you asking?" I say, because even though I'm not sure what he's thinking, I can't help flirting back.

He leans back in the chair and gives me a shrug I take to mean *Why not?*

"Well, grab a book and read," I say. "Or do whatever it is you do when you usually come in here and I'll draw you." I give him a smile I'm sure he thinks is beyond dopey. I have to cover the fact that my hand is shaky somehow, though.

"All right. I usually come here just to sit in front of the fire. You know, to get away from my parents for a while. But I can find a book. Or we can talk, if you can draw and talk at the same time."

"Um, I can't draw as well if you're watching me back. I have a thing about that." That's a lie, because I usually can. I've listened to my chemistry teacher drone on and on about neutrons and protons and atomic numbers, yet still manage to sketch him standing behind his monster desk and then ace the exam the next day. But Georg is throwing me off. "It might be better if you read."

I start to draw, and get about halfway done when he suddenly looks at his watch and says something under his breath in German.

"Have to go?" Maybe I took too long. Or maybe he only asked me to draw him so he'd have someone to talk to, and me not talking is boring him out of his skull.

"My parents expect me to have dinner with them, and I'm late." He looks unhappy about leaving, which makes me feel better. I mean, it's nice when an intriguing guy wants to stay and sit with you. People who look like Christie never appreciate it, because it happens to them all the time. But me, I appreciate it.

"Sorry," I say. "Didn't mean to—"

"If you'd like, I can come at the same time tomorrow. I need something to do. Before my parents find something for me to do. I don't think it's occurred to them that I'm on break yet."

"I hear you. I'm sure I'll be here. My dad's making me study for some exams I have to take before I start school."

He stands up, and I realize that Georg's pretty tall. Probably six feet. I sooo love tall. "I can help you if you need to know anything," he offers. "You'll be in year ten, right?"

"If that's what you call tenth grade."

He grins. "I'm in year eleven, so I had all your teachers last year. Just ask if you have any questions, and I'll give you the dish." When he says "dish," he hesitates, like he's not quite sure that's the right word to use.

I let it slide. "Thanks. That'd be cool."

I look down at the picture in my lap once he's gone. I'll have no problem finishing it in my room tonight. Georg has a face that's great to draw—really high cheekbones, blue eyes, and fair skin. And he's got this dark, dark hair with just the slightest curl to it. There's a lot I can do with shading when I sketch someone like him. Lots of contrast to play around with.

I pile up all the textbooks, still unopened, and drag myself out of the comfy chair and back toward the so-called apartment. I might not have gotten any studying done, but I feel a lot better. Georg's absolutely delicious, even if he is David's polar opposite, lookswise, and he has a grown-up edge to him that makes me suspect he'd look down on me if he knew the real me—the me who stands behind Wendy's with my buds and sneaks cigarettes, or who stands in the corner at school dances and mocks the cheerleaders with their supertight, belly button–baring tops and overprocessed hair. (Okay, I mostly do this because no one ever asks me to dance, so I have nothing else to do. I'll admit it.)

Or the me with a lesbian mother and a father who, while totally straight, knows the proper way to serve beluga caviar and which style wineglass to use for a cabernet versus a white zinfandel.

But I'm happy anyway, because I can tell Georg's going to be a lot more interesting to hang out with than David ever was.

Georg likes my sketches. And he actually *talks* to me, unlike David.

Okay, I take that back. David does talk to me. But it's not like he sets a time and a place when he says, "See you tomorrow." There's a difference.

I can't wait to see if my computer's hooked up so I can tell Christie I won't be totally friendless in Schwerinborg.

Or not.

I'll have to think about it first.

Five

To: ChristieT@viennawest.edu
From: Val@realmail.sg.com
Subject: Official Schwerinborg Palace E-mail
(AS IF!)

Hey, Christie!

Told you it wasn't like you'd never talk to me again. Less than 24 hours and here I am in your face already.

So here's the latest: I really am living in a palace. Not the fairy-tale kind with turrets—this one's more like a big mansion. There are lots of paintings of old men on the walls in the main part of the palace, and each and every one of these guys looks constipated. You'd think they'd get more fiber. Or, assuming they didn't have Metamucil handy, that the artists wouldn't immortalize them in oils looking so pained (and no goofing on how you think I make *you* look constipated, okay? I so *don't*.).

What really rots, though, is that my room feels like it's in Antarctica instead of Schwerinborg. You'd think that royalty could afford heat, but Dad tells me that European palaces constructed in the 1700s have their limitations.

The government offices—in a different part of the palace, next to where Prince Manfred lives—were done over in the mid 90s and are all beautiful and modern on the inside. Those rooms have heat. Of course.

That's it for now—I want to make sure this gets through before I type any more. If it does, you HAVE to tell me how things went last night at David's Christmas party. Did David actually get booze like Jeremy said he would? Did you drink anything? I just know I'd chicken out. I mean, how'd you get back in your house? My parents would smell alcohol on my breath from a mile away.

And—most important—any south-of-the-border action with Jeremy?

Needless to say, I have not met a single David Anderson look-alike yet, so your dreams of someday double dating with me and the real David (ha ha ha!!) are safe. If I have to judge by the looks of the guys who carried our luggage up to our rooms, I'm not expecting Schwerinborg to be Hottie Heaven. But I'll let you know if anything develops.

Val

After firing off my e-mail to Christie, I send slightly blander e-mails to Jules and Natalie, just so they won't feel unloved. I'm exhausted, but I just know that if Christie gets an e-mail tonight and Jules and Natalie don't get any until tomorrow, they'll get all whiny and overanalyze the whole thing, decide I've turned into a total bitch, and then they'll refuse to e-mail me back out of spite.

Of course, it won't even occur to them that they've ignored me for, like, the last *week.*

Sometimes girls suck. Guys would never be this way.

I probably should have told Christie

about Georg, but—since, even though I adore her, Christie is a typical girly-girl too and overanalyzes everything—I'm afraid it'll make her think I'm not interested in David. And I still want to hear how, or *if,* David says anything to Jeremy about me being gone, before I say anything about Georg.

Plus, I figure I should wait and see if my first impression of Georg holds up before I announce that I've found a potential friend—maybe even a boyfriend—over here. Telling anyone would be making my expectations official, and I'm not there yet.

I curl up in bed, hug my pillow (a rather flat and hard thing—I may have to add *fluffy pillow* to *hair dryer* on the shopping list), and try to go to sleep. You'd think, given the fact that I've been up for a bazillion hours trying to regulate my body to European time, that I'd crash hard. But I can't. I'm obsessing over David.

I pull my pillow closer and wonder what it'd be like if it was David cuddling with me instead. Would his blond hair feel as soft as it looks when I'm sitting behind him at a football game? Would he hold me tight, with his body fitting right against mine, and tell me that he's loved me from afar for years and been too scared to say so?

I know it's impossible, but late at night, when I'm alone in bed, I can't help but pretend.

As my mind drifts, I find myself wondering what might have happened if I could have gone to David's Christmas party, and if my mom was her old self and I didn't have to give a rat's ass about David's dad and his beliefs. Would David and I have ended up making out in some bedroom or on the back porch, like Jeremy and Christie always do?

Of course, I've never seen south-of-the-border action, like I suspect Christie and Jeremy might have if they got enough privacy after the party ended last night. I haven't even seen *north*-of-the-border action. Christie suspects this, but I haven't told her for sure. Even though the A-listers know I've never had a serious boyfriend, I've tried to be real mysterious about what happens on family vacations or who I might've met when I had to go to summer camp during junior high. I don't want them to think I'm a total loser.

And besides, they're not going to tell me about *their* action if they think I won't get what they're talking about. But how can I get it—or get any, really—if they won't tell me anything? How else am I going to figure it all out so I don't make a complete and total fool of myself when a guy really does get interested?

I fold my pillow in half so it's almost like my pillow at home and close my eyes. But the second I get comfortable, there's a light knock on my door and I hear Dad whisper, "Val? You still awake?"

I take a deep breath and debate turning up the Avril Levigne playing on my clock radio. Finally I just click it off and answer, "Yeah. What's up, Dad?"

He opens the door, and enough light comes in from the living room to make me squint when I look in his direction. I think he's holding my notebook, but it's hard to tell. "Valerie, I'm sorry to wake you up. I hope you don't think this is an invasion of your privacy, but I needed a piece of paper, and—"

He reaches for the light switch, but I

wave for him to quit. "Hey! No lights!"

He hesitates, then leans against the door frame. "Did you draw this picture?"

"If it's in that notebook, then yeah, probably. Hold it out in the light and I'll tell you for sure."

He takes a step back into the living room and holds up the notebook, which is opened to the page with my half-finished picture of Georg.

"Yeah," I say. "His name's Georg. He came into the library after I went down there to study. He introduced himself, and we talked for a while."

"Did he see you drawing this?"

I push myself up on my elbows and shrug. "It was his idea. Why? What's the big deal?"

"What do you know about this young man?"

I can't believe he woke me up for this. Or almost woke me up, at least.

"Geez, Dad, chill. There's nothing to get in a twist about. His parents work here in the palace, so he lives here, like us. We were just hanging out in the library, that's all. I promise. I sat up straight and acted like a good girl and everything."

Dad sucks in a deep breath, and even in the half light streaming in from the living room, I can see his nostrils going in, then out. "Did Georg tell you what his parents do?"

"Does it matter?"

Dad takes a step into my room. "Yes. Because Georg is *Prince Georg,* Valerie. Prince Manfred is Georg's father. You didn't know that?"

Um, no, I didn't know that, so I just stare at my dad. I mean, the idea never even occurred to me. For one, that there were *any* kids in the palace, let alone that Prince Manfred might have a son my age— though now that I think about it, Dad did say Manfred had a kid who goes to the American school. Anyway, for two, even if I *had* known, who'd believe a prince would wander into the library and just start talking to me? Or that he'd know my name even before he came in?

I mean, *come on.*

Georg cannot be a prince. Wrong, wrong, wrong. He would have said something, wouldn't he? Especially since, if it *is* true, and he really *is* a prince, then by definition, he is the Coolest Guy in School. Numero uno, supersnob, and guaranteed prom king. And way, way too popular to have been hanging out in the library on the wrong side of the palace with Yours Truly. A guy like that would have made it crystal clear within two seconds of introducing himself that he was in his league, and I was in mine, even if we were now living under the same roof.

Oh, man. I bet he knows William and Harry. THAT William and Harry. He probably hangs with them on his school vacations and they ride horses or play polo or whatever snooty sport rich kids play. 'Cause if Georg's a prince, that means he has more money than I could ever hope to count. He goes to all the best parties. He's probably even been to raves with ultralean, ultrasexy European supermodels.

I have not been to a rave. Ever. And neither have my boring, just-cool-enough-not-to-get-picked-on friends.

What I *have* done is make a total ass of myself, acting so high and mighty sitting in *his* library. Telling him his country is *gray* and *boring*, while I live in a tiny little part of his father's palace where I eat McChicken on a Formica table and sit on a chair with unbalanced legs.

My dad is going to kill me if he finds out what I said.

At least I didn't tell Georg that most of my friends don't know the difference between Schwerinborg and a smorgasbord. As if I didn't make a big enough idiot of myself to start with.

"You didn't know, did you?" my dad asks again, though he can tell what the answer is from my face, so I don't even bother with the Valerie Shrug.

"I'm glad you met someone your age," he adds in his I'm-your-dad-and-I-love-you voice, which means a *but* is sure to follow. And it did. "But you need to be careful with Georg. Remember when you were seated at the White House picnic last year with the Carew boys? Same thing applies here."

I roll my eyes. Dad lectured me in the car the whole way to that picnic. I wasn't to talk to the Carew twins—two megaspoiled freshmen who think they're God's gift—about anything personal. As if I would. I can't stand the Carews. Not because of politics, either. They're just revolting as people.

And Dad's lecture didn't matter anyway, because the Carews had no intention of talking to me. In fact, they made a point of ignoring me so I'd *know* I was being ignored. Jerks.

"Dad"—I look him in the eye to make sure he knows he's being ridiculous—"I'm not going to give Georg your credit card number or tell him you smoked pot in college or anything."

"Not only is that not funny, you know it's not true." He turns on the light, but since I'm totally awake now, I don't argue this time. I yank my feet up closer to my body so he can sit on the edge of my bed. When he does, he grabs one of my feet through the covers and wiggles it around, just like he did when I was a kid and I told him there was a dragon in my bed and he had to catch it before it ate my foot.

"Val, it's not that I think you're spilling your guts to a stranger. I know you're good about keeping our family matters private, but I just thought I'd give you a word of warning. That's all. We're new here, and Georg's father is my boss. So let's keep our ears and eyes open and learn our way around, all right?"

I nod. I'm a listen-first-speak-second kind of person, anyway.

"Georg's an okay guy though, isn't he?" I ask a few minutes later, after Dad pesters me about whether I got any studying done. Maybe Dad knows something about Georg. He hears all the dish about politicians, celebrities, and their kids, and he usually even knows which rumors are true.

"As far as I know, Prince Georg's fine. He's supposed to be quite intelligent, and he's never gotten into any kind of trouble that would embarrass his family . . . like smoking cigarettes. Or pot." He says this with a funny look that makes me wonder if he's joking, or if he's really thinking *I* might be taking the occasional drag at parties since I made the wisecrack about him doing it.

"Well, that's good," I say, not willing to give an inch. I've *never* smoked that stuff and Dad should know it. My grades are too important to me. Besides, I got in enough trouble just getting caught with cigarettes last year. Getting busted with a joint would be something else entirely, especially if I got arrested. Thanks but no thanks.

"I'll leave you alone then," he says, giving my foot one last squeeze before walking to the door. I burrow back under the covers, but just before he shuts off the light, he turns around. "Valerie?"

"Yeah?"

"You have a lot of talent. I wish you'd shown me your drawings yourself."

"They're okay," I say, but secretly I'm glad he likes them. Dad has taste, and he doesn't give compliments easily.

"Have you ever shown them to your mother?"

"No."

"Oh." He stares at the sketch of Georg, and I realize he thinks this is a real bonding moment. He knows something about me that Mom doesn't.

Then, of course, he ruins it by going and suggesting art lessons.

"Dad—" I shoot him my best warning stare before he gets going about all the access I'll have to great teachers here in Schwerinborg. He should remember that piano lessons killed any and all interest I had in the piano. There's no way I'd do that to my sketches. Even if I never do end up making a career of it, what would I do to get through AP English every day?

"Okay. Just a suggestion." Then his eyes get a mischievous look. "But I bet Georg would be really impressed if you got his chin just right. Art lessons would help."

He walks off before I can hit him in the head with the nearest baseball-sized object, which happens to be my alarm clock. Lucky for him.

He is so not funny.

I'm in the middle of looking over the formula for determining molar volume—which means I'm mostly thinking about how much I hate chemistry—when I finally hear what I've been listening for. Someone at the door to the library.

Refusing to look anxious, I keep right on scribbling down the formula.

I do *not* want Georg to know I've been

thinking about him for, oh, the last fifteen hours straight. I bet he gets a lot of that. Like, from every single female in school.

I still can't figure out why he even bothered to say hello to me, let alone ask if he could hang with me in the library again today.

"Fraulein Winslow?"

I jump about a mile. The guy standing behind me is definitely not who I was expecting. He's about fifty years too old to be Georg, and his voice sounds like he's been chain-smoking since he was seven. I wouldn't want my voice to sound like that even if I was a hundred. I make a mental note to limit my emergency smoking to a pack a *year,* if that.

"I hope I did not disturb you." The man smiles. He's got gray hair and a potbelly that sticks straight out. He looks more pregnant than fat. But he's wearing a nice suit, and he's smiling, so I figure he's okay, even if he did call me a *fraulein* and has such a thick accent I can barely understand him. Plus, this section of the palace isn't exactly open to the world. There's a metal detector and a fleet of security guards to get through first.

"No. May I help you?" I ask. Dad would like that I'm being all formal and polite.

"My name is Karl Oberfeld," he says, "but you may call me Karl. Your father mentioned that you are spending today in study, so I thought I might bring you some refreshment—a Coke and some pretzels, perhaps?"

I sit up straighter. "Um, sure. But you don't have to. I mean, I can get my own from my apartment." It still feels weird referring to a group of rooms with Holiday Inn decor as an *apartment,* but Dad assures me that's what it is.

"It would be my pleasure to bring you a snack from the kitchen." I can tell from his expression that he thinks it's odd that I want to get my food myself, so I tell him okay, I'll take a Coke and pretzels, but to make it a Diet Coke.

Of course, when he walks away, I realize I should have said *Coke Light.* I sound like such an American. It's kind of embarrassing.

So a few minutes later, when I hear footsteps again, I turn around expecting

Karl. Of course, *now* it's Georg. And of course, I'm looking desperate, since the very mention of Diet Coke has made me really thirsty.

"How's the studying going?" Georg asks. I just wave at my books with a you-know-how-it-goes flip of my hand. He takes the chair next to me, but seems a little hesitant, as if he's afraid he's interrupting. I have to wonder: Why does everyone always seem to feel uncomfortable here? Like they're *bothering* you just by wanting to talk. Is this a palace thing?

"You don't have to memorize all those for the exams"—he jerks his head toward the formulas scribbled on my notebook page—"they give them to you. They just want to see if you've learned to apply them."

I can't help but groan in total disgust. "You're kidding, right? I've been trying to pound these into my brain all over again."

"You're better off not studying at all, I think." He leans forward as he says this, and there's a cute little twinkle in his eyes, like I'm amusing him. "Though I'm sure my parents would make me study too."

I laugh. He might be a prince, but he's cool. I hadn't thought about it, but I suppose it wouldn't look good for Prince Manfred and Princess Claudia if their only son flunked out of school. It'd probably be all over the *National Enquirer.* Or the *Schwerinborg Enquirer,* if there's such a thing. So much for Georg living a total life of luxury.

"I don't know what it is," I say, "but as soon as I finish an exam, all the formulas I have to memorize for it go right out of my head. I figure that if I get a job in a lab someday, no one's going to care if I open up a book and look up a freaking formula. Besides, since I'd be using them everyday, and I wouldn't have to worry about learning stuff for five or six other classes at the same time, I'd memorize them whether I wanted to or not."

"Exactly!" He's giving me that slow, sexy smile again, and it's like we have this scary-weird-cool connection. Then he adds, "Not that I want to be a scientist. I think it'd be about the most boring job in the world. Or, at least, it would be for me," he says, covering, and I can tell he's worried that I'm secretly dreaming of becoming a rocket scientist and he might have offended me. "Is it something you think you'd find interesting?"

"No way!" I laugh again, even though all this giggling is probably making me sound like one of those bimbettes who goes on *The Bachelor*. Eeww. I compensate by telling him, "My science grades have always been really good, all A's, but there are things I'd rather do with my life."

"Like what?"

I hesitate. Telling him I want to sketch for a living would make me look like I'm too stupid to do anything *real*. Like be a lawyer or an architect or run my own business or something, which is what my parents want and expect. But I just can't get myself psyched up for anything like that. Not yet.

"I'm still thinking about it," I finally say. "Most of my friends' older brothers and sisters seem like they change their minds once they get to college, so I'm trying not to get too focused on any one thing until then."

"So what will you major in?"

"Nothing that has to do with science, that's for sure," I joke. "But I've got two more years to figure it out. You're a junior, though. So what about you?"

Of course, as soon as the question is out of my mouth, I think, *Duh, Valerie!* The dude's got his future all mapped out. He's going to rule a country! He's going to major in economics or political science or something like that, and then he'll work in some government job until his father kicks off.

I am amazed by how stupid I can be sometimes.

Thankfully I am saved by my dear buddy Karl. Apparently Georg saw Karl in the hall and told the old guy what he wanted too, 'cause Karl has a Diet Coke for me, a Coke for Georg, and a mondo-sized bowl of pretzels. He also has a few cut-up sandwiches on a tray, which make my tummy start to rumble the minute I see them.

I can get used to service like this.

Karl gives Georg a little bow, then leaves the room. A *bow*. Georg must think, judging from my idiotic question, that I'm a disrespectful smart-ass.

"If I could be anything at all," Georg says, handing me a sandwich on a little plate, "I think I'd be a professional soccer player."

"Really? Do you play a lot?" It occurs to me that it's probably rude to ask, since I'm guessing most Schwerinborgians (if that's what they're called—I'll have to check with Dad—maybe it's *Schwerinborgers* or just *the Borg,* like on *Star Trek*) would automatically know this kind of trivia about their prince. But since this is the way I talk with my friends, and Georg's never actually come out and *told* me he's a prince—and doesn't seem to want me to know, judging from the way he was uncomfortable with Karl bowing to him in front of me—I decide to just be my laid-back, friendly self, and so what if he thinks I'm rude.

Although my laid-back, friendly self was also of the opinion that someone with Georg's background would dream of a sport that involves horses and where he has to wear jodhpurs. Not *soccer.* My bad.

"I play indoor soccer all year. And at school I made varsity on the outdoor team my freshman year." He says it without bragging, simply as a statement of fact. "I had to work pretty hard to do it, though. I was certain I'd get busted back to the JV team after every single game."

"But you weren't, were you?"

He shakes his head between sips of Coke, and his cheeks get pink. It's totally cute.

"Next year, when I'm a senior, I hope I'm the captain. I'd really like to play pro for a year or two before I go to college." He glances up at the fireplace, where there's an oil painting showing a woman who's probably one of his ancestors. She's wearing a high collar, and looks just as constipated as all the old guys whose portraits are hanging in the halls. For a minute, I wonder if Georg will ever sit for one, and if the artist will be obliged to make him look just as cramped.

He looks away from the picture at the same time I do, then takes another long swig of his Coke. "There's no way my parents will allow it. They want me to go straight through school."

"Mine too," I agree as soon as I swallow

my bite of sandwich. I don't know what magic Karl has worked on these things— they're filled with your basic deli turkey, cucumbers, and a sauce I don't recognize— because they're phenomenal. "I never thought of doing anything else, though. But maybe if I was good at something like soccer, I would."

He doesn't say anything, so I wonder for a minute if he's kind of depressed about the soccer thing. Maybe if I apologize for calling Schwerinborg gray and boring yesterday, it'll remind him of how much he likes living here and cheer him up a little.

But then he'd know I know he's the prince.

I may have to ask Dad about how to handle this point of etiquette, though I don't want to let on to Dad that I get along with Georg so well. Dad will get all jumpy about it, and I don't want to get Georg in trouble either. I get the feeling he hasn't told anyone about his soccer dream. Or at least not his parents, and I don't want Dad to let on to them. Parents talk, as Jules, Natalie, Christie, and I discovered after Jules's mom saw us hanging out with a group of high school boys at the 7-Eleven during our lunch hour when we were all in eighth grade. I didn't get to go to that 7-Eleven again for almost a year, my parents were so sure that I was going to hook up with some older guy who might, in Dad's words, "take advantage of my youth." As if. We never even found out all those guys' names.

"So what do you do for fun around here?" I ask. "Besides hang out in the library, I mean."

He gives me a smile that makes my stomach freeze. It's bizzaro—he's not *that* good looking. At least not classically, every-girl-would-die good looking. There's an edge to him that takes him out of total hottie contention. Still . . .

Maybe I'm just lonely is all.

"I don't, usually," he says, grabbing another of Karl's sandwiches. "I play soccer, I go to the movies. Stuff like that. But it's vacation time now, and my parents both have stuff scheduled they couldn't re-arrange, so we couldn't go anywhere this year."

"You wouldn't rather hang with your friends?"

One of his eyebrows shoots up. "Who says you're not a friend?"

Six

"Thanks." I try not to look taken off guard, but it's kind of cool, being called a friend by a freakin' *prince.* Especially since I can tell he actually means it. At least, I hope he does, because otherwise, I'm pretty much friendless here. It's a pretty safe assumption that if Georg decides he doesn't like me, I'm basically screwed at school. No one's going to want to be buddy-buddy with the girl the prince says is a total reject. And I wouldn't blame them either. *I'd* even ignore me.

"I would guess you have other friends besides me, though," I tell him, mostly to cover my own stupid smiley face reaction to what he said. I don't want Georg to think I'm desperate, because I'm not. Being an only child makes me tough that way, or so I tell myself. "Unless you're, like, a known ax murderer or something, and you're just being nice to lull me into a false sense of security."

He holds his hands over his head, outlaw-style, then leans back in his chair, kicking his long legs closer to me. "You've caught me. I admit it. I'm sure the police will have my . . ." He fumbles for the right phrase for a second before saying, "My mug shot stapled to all the telephone poles soon."

He glances over his shoulder, toward the door, then shoots a casual look at my notebook. "You still have that drawing from yesterday?"

Does he not want his family to know I'm drawing him? Instead of asking him about it, I make a quick resolution to shut the notebook if his parents—or anyone— shows up, just in case.

"Oh, now I get it," I say as I turn to the correct notebook page. "You only want me around long enough to draw a flattering wanted poster for you." Why not tease him like I would a normal friend, I figure, since he doesn't know I know who he really is? "I assume you're asking because you want me to finish?"

"I'd like that a lot. But don't make my head too big."

"I'll draw it like I see it," I retort. He grins, and for the next few minutes, we're quiet. I take my time with shading and getting the angle of his jaw just so. Since this one's on request, as opposed to my usual killing-time-in-homeroom job, I want it to be really good.

And I have to admit, I'm getting a Zen feeling sitting with him, not saying anything and just drawing. I wouldn't have guessed I'd be so comfortable with anyone who thinks in German, no matter how good his English might be. It's relaxing, like when I'm with Christie, Jules, or Natalie. They're the only people who seem to get that it's okay to hang out and not talk sometimes. To just *be*.

At least until I told them I was moving to Schwerinborg.

When I finish and hold up the picture,

I can't believe how happy Georg looks. Not goofy happy. Touched happy.

"That's awesome, Valerie." His accent nearly cracks me up. It's like talking to the Terminator or something. But I manage to keep a straight face.

"It's all yours." I rip out the page and hand it to him, but he makes me sign it first.

I cannot believe *I* am autographing something for *him*. It's just wrong.

"I know you have to take the first placement exams tomorrow," he says, his eyes still focused on the picture. "And I'm going to be busy for a few days after that. I have some, um, family things my parents need me to attend. But I'll look for you before school starts, okay?"

"That'd be great, Georg." It's surreal, talking to someone who's not only a prince, but is named *Georg*. He really should be Scott or Josh or something. But as surreal as it is, I feel like he's invited me into his world.

Once he's out of the library, though, and I'm by myself with the leftover pretzels and sandwiches, I can't help but wonder how long it'll last. Maybe Georg's parents told him to be nice to me. Or maybe he's just bored to death being stuck at home over break and would rather crash in the library with a geeky sophomore than do nothing at all.

I wonder when the bomb's going to drop. Maybe the first week of school. Will he totally start ignoring me? Will he wake up and realize I'm a geek?

Or worse, is he going to drop little hints to his friends that I'm all in love with him so he can look like he's gotten some action over break? Part of me knows this is ridiculous. I mean, he doesn't set off my bullshit detector at all, and I can detect a bullshitter nine times out of ten. But I've seen more than one guy pull that particular trick, especially in the case of older guys talking about a girl who's a couple years younger, so it's not beyond the realm.

As I leave the library I decide my new mission is to find out more about him. Not so I can replace my David Anderson look-alike mission, but so I don't show up at school and find out that no one—David look-alike or not—will have anything to do with me because Georg really is lulling me into a false sense of security.

At least David never did anything like that.

Still, I'm getting tired of having the things I count on in life ripped away from me. And for whatever pathetic, needy reason, I really, really want to count on Georg. I want to believe in the scary-weird-cool connection thing.

Because what if?

To: Val@realmail.sg.com
From: ChristieT@viennawest.edu
Subject: Hottie Heaven

Hey, Val Pal!

Sorry it's taken me a couple days to get back to you. But you would NOT believe what's happened here. Let's just say that there wasn't even CLOSE-to-the-border action with Jeremy, let alone anything *SOUTH* of the border, because David's parents decided to stay in the house during the Christmas party. We all pretty much sat around watching videos and drinking this dumb fruit punch his mom made. Booorrring.

Aside from the videos, about all we did was talk about you. Get this: David said he looked up the Schwerinborg royal family on the Web, and he found all these pictures of them and their palace! Jeremy and I went with Jules into David's room to look on the computer during the party. Val, I don't care how cold you think it is, or whether there are turrets, it looks like a fairy tale!

And you totally lied when you said that Schwerinborg isn't Hottie Heaven. I mean, have you been able to see Prince Georg yet? Apparently, there's a sixteen- (almost seventeen) year-old prince in Schwerinborg. And he's TOTALLY HOT!!! You'll have to tell me if he looks as good in real life if you actually see him. Wouldn't that be something, to see a real prince? Although Georg is kind of a funny name. Do all people in Schwerinborg have weird names like that? Wasn't that the name of the father in *The Sound of Music*?

Anyway, when I said Georg looked like a hottie, David got all weird and clicked on another picture, one that showed the palace's dining room or something. I think he was jealous! It was sooo cute. No one else picked up on it, not even Jeremy, who you'd think wouldn't want me looking at David so closely. But I swear, it's true. And what was David doing looking up Schwerinborg in the first place if he wasn't interested in you??

My cousins are visiting from Tennessee, so my mom's making us all go to the Smithsonian with them. AND we have to do the White House tour. Y-a-w-n.

I'll e-mail you in a couple days, after they're GONE. But write me again soon. You're the best friend I've ever had, and I miss you lots!!

Hugs and love, Christie

PS—My mom says if you have a phone number you can give me, that she MIGHT let me call you, but it can only be ten minutes because it's expensive, and only if I'm nice to my cousins. SO GIVE ME YOUR NUMBER!!

I've been sick to my stomach all day. No one told me how hard it is to go to a new school.

You'd think, being fifteen, I'd be past all this first-day-of-school-nervousness crap. I'm so *not*. First, I now realize how incredibly sheltered I've been, attending the same school system since preschool. I mean, living in northern Virginia means we get kids moving in and out every year, because there are so many diplomats, military parents, you name it, who move all the time. It's just the nature of being around D.C. But I've never had to move.

And now I'm realizing just how much it sucks walking into a school with a few hundred high schoolers and not knowing ANYONE.

Well, anyone except Georg. And I haven't seen him in over a week, since right before I had to take my placement exams.

Second, I'm having a major guilt trip over each and every new kid at school I've ever ignored. Images of kid after kid who tried to say hi to me are coming back, and I'm thinking I'm going to lose my lunch of (get this!) sauerbraten and carrot salad every single time I think of another face. It's not that I was mean to anyone. I was always nice and said hello back. I just didn't go out of my way to make sure they had someone to sit next to at lunch.

Which is probably why I spent my

lunch hour sitting completely, totally alone. God is getting back at me.

I felt like the world's biggest butt-wipe, sitting at a cafeteria table eating sauerbraten—which is beyond gross—while all the kids around me yakked about going skiing in Switzerland or shopping in Paris over their Christmas break. I wasn't about to try to introduce myself—again—and tell them that I got to visit the Louvre once. With my *parents*. It'd be like stamping *L-O-S-E-R* in big red letters right across my forehead.

Or however you spell it in German.

On the other hand, classes aren't as bad as I thought. My desk in Western Civilization, where I'm currently sitting, and sketching, is a bit wobbly. But the teachers really are Americans, like Dad promised. Most of them seem to be younger than my teachers at Vienna West too, maybe in their twenties. And they're all *fun.* I mean, when your Western Civ teacher draws a big picture across the chalkboard showing what a pillory looks like, or talks for fifteen minutes about the various disgusting ways suspected witches were tried in medieval times, it's entertaining in a whacked sort of way. Way more cool than listening to Mrs. Bennett lecture in a monotone about the ramifications of the Emancipation Proclamation.

And actually getting to live where all this stuff took place is making it interesting too. Apparently we're going to get to go on field trips to two different art museums this quarter. And we get to take a bus to a place called Rothenburg, in Germany, to see a museum that's completely dedicated to medieval punishments.

Is that not wild?

Still, I'm really glad this is the last class of the day. I don't know why, since it's only three o'clock, but I'm wiped. All I want to do is go home and check my e-mail. Maybe even try to talk Dad into making some magic with his pots and pans. I'm thinking something fried and fatty and totally unhealthy, since I'm never going to have to worry about the size of my thighs or butt again. Judging from today, I may as well be invisible, so there's no way I'm ever going to have a boyfriend.

When the bell rings, I can't get out fast

enough. But the minute my way-too-American-looking shoes hit the cobble-stoned street, I feel it.

I'm starting my period.

I usually go gangbusters on my first day, so an instant wave of panic is more than warranted. I find a bench next to the sidewalk, sit down (carefully!), and rummage through my backpack, hoping that I still have something stashed in the inside pocket from last semester.

Of course, I don't.

I get up and half run, half walk (so I don't look too anxious as I pass by everyone who's leaving) back into the school. Unfortunately the girls' bathroom is no help either. No machines on the wall. Now what? There's no way I'm going to stick my nose into the group of snotty girls standing just outside the bathroom and ask if I can borrow something. If I do, for the next year it'll be, like, "Oh, yeah, I met Valerie Winslow. She was the girl who asked me for a Tampax her first day of school."

Um, thanks but no thanks.

I'm about to race to the nurse's office—

I assume there's a nurse's office, but I don't know, which means I'm going to have to embarrass myself further by asking in the main office—when I see a basket on the shelf next to the mirrors.

I peek inside. Halle-freakin'-lujah. At least one thing is going to go right today.

A few minutes later, I'm back outside. Of course, half the kids are still hanging around the outside doors, and the ones who saw me bolting out of class and not bothering to stop at my locker the first time I left school are looking at me now, probably wondering what I was doing back in the building.

I yank my backpack a little farther up my shoulder, put my head down, and blow past them. I want nothing more than to be out of here. Maybe I'll have some e-mail from the A-listers. Something more about David and him being jealous would suit me just fine right now.

Luckily it's not a real long walk home—to the palace, that is. It only takes about ten or fifteen minutes. But there's also a streetcar stop right by the school, and if I hop on, it's only one stop to get to the palace. Since the streetcar is pulling up, and Dad bought me a pass yesterday, I jump on. I punch my ticket in the little yellow machine on board and congratulate myself on figuring out something about Schwerinborg without having Dad tell me.

I quickly realize that this is a mistake, because the second the streetcar starts moving, I wobble, fall onto one of the bench seats, and nearly end up in this old lady's lap. She's in an all-black dress, and she has on—no, I'm not kidding—knee-high nylons, and you can see the tops of them at the hem of her dress. And her legs are all hairy, too.

She waves me off and says something in German that doesn't sound particularly civil, but I have no idea what. And no idea how to apologize. I make an *I'm so sorry* face as I stand up from the too-narrow space beside her, go to the other side of the car, and grab on to an empty pole.

This shouldn't upset me. But it does.

I can feel tears in my eyes, burning way at the back, and I blink to keep myself calm. I so need Jules and Natalie. They'd have made me laugh with some offhand crack about how the Schwerinborgers need an introduction to Nair. Or Christie, who'd have said something miraculous to the old woman to make it all better.

I sure hope Christie got my e-mail with my phone number, and that her mom lets her call me tonight instead of waiting for the weekend. I'm going to go over the edge if I have to wait until Friday to talk to someone about all this.

I mentally pray that Christie will be extra nice to her Tennessee cousins and that they all have a fabulouso time at the Smithsonian. I'm desperate.

Then I hear this voice near me speaking German, but it's familiar. *Way* familiar.

"You okay?" Georg asks in English when I turn around.

"Um, yeah," I manage, wondering if my day could possibly go any further downhill. I know how bad I look when I get into almost-crying mode. Before I can take two seconds and think, I blurt out, "What are you doing here?"

"I saw you getting on the *strassenbahn* and decided to follow you."

"Saw me making a total dork of myself."

I give the woman I tripped over a weak smile, but she's just staring at Georg.

"I told her it was an accident, and that you're a very nice person but that you don't speak German."

"Or know how to stand up on a *strassenbahn*," I say, trying out the German word for "streetcar." "But thanks."

I think I'm turning red now.

Georg puts his hand on my lower back, and the feel of his fingers through my clothes makes me freak out inside. "We're here."

I look out the window, and sure enough, we're slowing down alongside a street-level platform. There's a canopy over part of it, and in big black letters it says SCHLOSS, which Georg tells me is the German word for "castle."

Schloss doesn't sound like a castle to me, but seeing as the rear gate to the palace is across the street, I trust him that it doesn't mean "sewage treatment plant," which would've been my guess.

I still can't believe that a prince is on this thing. And from the looks other people are giving him—most are more discreet than the old lady, either peeking from behind newspapers or past grab bars—I'm guessing this isn't the usual way he comes home.

Once we're through the gate and we've climbed up the back stairs into the wing where my apartment is, Georg stops.

"What?" I frown. I'm about to apologize for screwing up on the streetcar, but he crooks his finger at me, then puts it over his lips. I follow him down a long hall, wondering what's with all the James Bond secrecy.

Oh, God. I hope I didn't have an accident. If there's a stain on my rear, and he's about to tell me, I am going to call my mom and go home to Virginia. Tomorrow.

No, tonight. I bet I can at least get to Munich tonight.

"Here," he whispers, then opens a door. I realize that we're on a balcony overlooking a huge reception hall. The floor below us is hardwood, with all these beautiful inlays. Big velvet curtains are hanging from windows that are almost two stories high, ending right below the balcony that circles the room. I feel like I've escaped from a

White House tour and stumbled into one of the secured areas.

"We're not supposed to be here, are we?"

"It's all right," he says. "But I wanted to get you alone so we could talk."

I start getting a creepy feeling. But excited, too, because he doesn't look upset or stressed, and I know I sure would be if I had to tell a girl she's been walking around with a big red spot on her pants.

This might even be something fun.

I eye the door we just entered through. "The library's not good enough?"

He shakes his head. "Karl will show up the minute we go in there. Or my father will, if he knows I'm home from school. He'll want me to tell him about my homework, what's due, all that. He keeps a very close eye on my assignments."

"That blows."

He lets out a little puff of air, kind of a half laugh. "Well, that's why I wanted to talk to you."

"About homework?"

"No. About the fact you say things like having my father watching me every second blows. You're . . . you're very normal."

"Thanks, I think." I'd rather he told me I'm hot, or maybe that I'm brilliant. At least that I'm a lot of fun. But I'll settle for normal.

"Trust me, it's a compliment." He drops down into one of the straight-backed chairs along the wall at the back of the balcony, and waves for me to do the same. I set my backpack down between my feet, then take the seat next to him.

"So what's up? You didn't need to talk to me alone about that, did you?"

He turns his head to look at me, and since we're less than an arm's length apart, I think I'm going to fall over. His eyes are just amazing. Not as good as David's—on the sparkly-cool scale, at least. But intense.

Georg takes a deep breath. "Do you know who I am, Valerie?"

"An ax murderer." It just pops out. I know he's trying to be serious, but I need *him* to tell me who he is.

He cracks up. "Would you have followed me in here if you believed that?"

"Not unless I had an ax of my own. And maybe a chainsaw."

He smiles, then props his elbows on his thighs and folds his hands in front of him. For a second he looks away from me and stares at his shoes. I want to tell him that for all his dark hair and serious expressions, he looks nothing like an ax murderer.

Or a prince. I mean, a prince who wears Levi's and rides the *strassenbahn*? A prince who hangs out with *moi*?

He told me I was normal.

I think I'm neurotic. He's probably the normal one.

I'm about to tell him this when he turns sideways in his chair and touches my hand. "I'm a prince. My dad's Prince Manfred." He looks up from where his hand is touching mine, and my heart stops cold the minute his eyes catch mine. "Did you know that, Valerie?"

Whoa.

"Yeah," I whisper. "I know. But I didn't. Not that evening when we first met in the library. I figured it out later."

"So how come you didn't say anything?"

I shrug, but all I can think about is how warm and strong his fingers are on mine. I wish they weren't. And I wish I didn't have such a thing about a guy's hands. It's distracting.

"I don't know," I finally answer. "You didn't say anything to me about it, so I figured it wasn't my business. That you'd tell me when you wanted to."

"But you didn't treat me any differently. You treated me like I was totally normal, even after you figured out who my parents are."

"Was I supposed to bow or something?" Okay, stop me *now*. He's going to think I'm the most evil, most smart-assed—

And then he kisses me.

Not a big, deep kiss, just a quick, soft kiss. Almost polite, but not quite. I mean, there's definitely more behind it than the David cheek kiss, and not just because this one's on the lips.

And the worst part is, it's over before I can even think about it.

"Um, I guess that's a no," I manage.

"It's definitely a no. I hate when people bow." He gives me this lopsided, embarrassed smile, and for a second I wonder if he's going to kiss me again. This time I'm definitely going to kiss back.

Definitely.

"I'm sorry," he says, and he shakes his head. "I probably shouldn't have done that."

I try not to let my mouth hang open. I'm stunned. Why the hell shouldn't he have done it? Because it's improper or something? Because I'm butt ugly and he had a momentary lapse of judgment?

Or because I totally screwed up the simplest kiss and he doesn't want me to think it's going to happen again, because there's no way on God's green earth his lips will ever come within a mile of my icky ones again?

He lets go of my hand and leans back in his chair, tilting on the rear legs so his shoulders are braced against the wall. "It's just . . . everyone I've ever met treats me differently. People who I know, just *know* in here"—he points to his chest—"don't really like me, but are always nice to me. I hate that. I hate that everyone is fake with me all the time. You're the only person I've ever met who's not."

I'm not sure what to say, so I just sit there looking like a total nimrod until he adds, "I just wanted to make sure you knew who I really am. Before you get to know everyone else at school, you know, and you see how they treat me and think that's how you have to treat me."

I'm trying to absorb what he's telling me, really. But all I can think about is the fact he kissed me, and what I can say to make him realize it wasn't a mistake.

"Hey, no problem," I say, "as long as all the people around here don't mind that I have no sense of what's proper"—I make a gesture encompassing the palace—"which is kind of funny, when you think about it, since knowing what's proper is my dad's whole job."

Georg laughs and stands up, so I do too. I guess in his mind, the conversation's over. There's this look of relief on his face, and I can actually feel the beat of my heart all the way in my ears.

And then he gives me a hug. It's all warm and tight and I can feel the muscles of his arms against my back.

Do people still swoon? Or is that considered out? 'Cause I feel a definite swoon coming on.

I start to turn my mouth toward his,

but before I can, he says, right into my ear, "Thanks, Valerie. You have no idea how much it means to me that I can be myself with you. I really want us to be good friends."

Seven

To: Val@realmail.sg.com
From: CoolJule@viennawest.edu
Subject: YOU

Hey Valerie,

You do know that you are living under the same roof as a prince named GEORG, don't you? And that his parents are named MANFRED and CLAUDIA? How whacked is THAT?!?!

While Claudia is okay (but only because of Claudia Schiffer), I think that Manfred is probably the stupidest name ever given to a human being. Fred is bad enough, but MAN-fred?? How did this guy survive childhood? If he was my brother, I'd have beat the crap out of him.

Anyway, I just wanted you to know I'm jealous as hell, because Georg looks like he'd be the best kisser in the universe. Track his gorgeous butt down and tell him I want to find out, okay? You're more than welcome to give him my e-mail address and phone number.

But don't tell him I work at Wendy's.

And write back to me soon. Vienna is the most boring place on the entire planet.

Jules

It takes supreme effort not to hit the delete key and pretend I never received Jules's e-mail, sort of because she apparently has the temporary hots for Georg, but especially because the way she and Natalie acted all pissy my last week in Virginia still has me a little torqued.

But since deleting isn't cool—I mean, she's still on my A list, and I guess I can understand her whole *Four Feathers* attitude, in a backward sort of way—my next urge is to ignore her until I get back from school and can say something intelligent about my new classes or some new friend I (probably won't) make or anything at all that has NOTHING to do with Georg, let alone how good a kisser he is.

That'd lead to a whole discussion of how awful I am at kissing, since I didn't even kiss him back, and I don't want to go there. I really want to talk to Christie first, but she didn't call and I simply *cannot* e-mail her with my whole Georg saga.

Some things just aren't for e-mail.

I stare at the screen for another minute before I click on the reply button. Since I know Jules always sends her e-mails with a return receipt requested, which means she knows who's opened her stuff and when, I can't blow her off. She'll check her e-mail first thing when she wakes up in the morning, and she'll know I didn't respond right away.

For being as tough as she is, Jules can be a real girly-girl about this kind of stuff.

To: CoolJule@viennawest.edu
From: Val@realmail.sg.com
Subject: RE: YOU

Hey, hey, Cool Jules!

You have no idea how awesome it was to wake up this morning to some friendly e-mail. Did Christie tell you how gray and boring this place is? It totally outbores Vienna. If it wasn't for Dad being lonely, I'd be home tomorrow. I miss you guys like mad.

And don't say you'd beat up Manfred for his name. One, you beat up your brother all the time, and his name's Mike, which is completely normal. Two, Manfred isn't bad looking, in an over-forty, dadish sort of way. Plus, I get the sense he wasn't the type of guy who let anyone push him around when he was a kid.

Sorry this is so short, but I have twenty minutes to make it to first period and it takes me fifteen minutes to get to school. More later!

Val

PS—I will not spread it around Schwerinborg that you work at Wendy's. But since I haven't even seen one here yet (sorry, only McDonald's and BK), I don't think they'd know what it is anyway.

★

I feel guilty as I shut off my computer. I've never out-and-out lied to Jules before. I mean, I know I didn't tell her the whole truth about my parents' divorce. I just left out the fact that my mom has a girlfriend. So it wasn't really a lie.

But this time I've *really* lied. I mean, this is right up there with Joe Millionaire not telling that he's flat broke (though some of those women deserved to be lied to). For one, Dad is *not* lonely—he's having a blast here, going to parties and meeting new people who take his mind off Mom. And for two, school doesn't start for over an hour. I just figure that if it sounds like I'm in a hurry, Jules won't notice that I blew off the whole Georg topic. Because I lied to Georg, too.

When he said he wanted to be friends, I told him that'd be *awesome.*

Yep, awesome. Right.

Apparently I'm a terrible liar, even when I don't open my mouth. Just *thinking* a lie is enough. I know this because Georg has obviously figured out that I'm crushing on him. He must have realized it even before I did, which was sometime last night while I was lying in bed, trying to focus on David and what Christie said about him being jealous, but really thinking about Georg.

Otherwise, if he hasn't figured this out, what was with kissing me and *then* giving me that whole "I really want us to be good friends" speech? And what was with him ignoring me on the way to school this morning? He left the palace at the same time I did, but walked about twenty steps ahead of me, acting like he hadn't seen me come out the side door.

I think he did, though.

It really bugs me, because after the whole hugging-just-friends thing, we had a great afternoon. I mean, we hid out in the balcony and talked for hours about what kind of music we like and how his parents have such impossible expectations of him. It turns out he has hardly any *real* friends, because the way things work for security reasons—and kind of for etiquette reasons—is that he always has to be the one to call his friends. They can't call him. And he sometimes wonders if his e-mail's monitored or his phone calls, since he uses the same phone line as his dad. So he just doesn't bother.

We also talked about Virginia, and my friends, and somehow we got going on skiing and snowboarding, and where we'd go on our dream trips. It was completely and totally cool. I had so much fun with him I even forgot about the kissing thing for a while.

Which is why the ignoring-me-on-the-way-to-school thing is messing with my mind. And it's still distracting me when lunch rolls around. There's open campus, but other than a little pizza window across the street and a nearby quickie mart (where all the crackers and premade sandwiches are labeled in German, which makes me suspicious of what's really inside) I don't see too many choices. Everyone is pretty much lingering near the school and doing whatever homework they have due this afternoon and still haven't finished.

Skipping the quickie mart, I backtrack to the cafeteria just long enough to buy a premade sandwich and a bag of chips— since here I can at least ask what's in the sandwich—then go back outside. No way do I want to sit alone at a long cafeteria table again. If I'm going to be alone, I want it less obvious.

Of course, I immediately see Georg out on the quad—the school's shaped like a horseshoe, and the area in the middle's called the quad even though it's not exactly square—and he must have eight other people hanging out with him. Maybe more. They're all so blindingly good looking I don't think I can watch them without damaging my retinas. He's grinning from ear to ear at this incredibly cute blond girl who's giggling at something he said, and of course he looks hotter than hot.

This is way worse than watching David Anderson and all his superathletic friends. Like, times a billion and one. David didn't talk to me very often, but at least he wouldn't have ignored me by walking ahead of me on the way to school. If he saw me, he'd have waited for me to catch up. He'd have kept right on talking to his jock friends for the most part, but still.

Georg catches my eye, and I almost wave, but he gets this *look,* then turns right back to the blonde, who doesn't even seem to notice the hitch in his conversation.

Then it hits me. He *knows.* He knows I'm into him and he doesn't want anyone to know he even knows who I am, let alone that he kissed me.

He seems so comfortable, yakking away with all his perfectly perfect buds, that all I can think is *Yeah, tell me again how you don't have any friends, Georg. Tell me again how awkward you feel all the time.* He sure doesn't look it—especially since he's all dressed up. Not really fancy—he's wearing jeans—but he's definitely a notch above everyone else. He's got on a soft, blue crew-neck sweater under this absolutely stunning black leather coat. It makes him look a lot older than sixteen.

There's not an ounce of doubt in my mind that this guy is going to be prom king when he's a senior. He's so popular, it's probably not even going to be a big deal to him, and I can't trust a guy who thinks that way.

I mean, the guy probably has a *real* crown hooked over his bedpost. And can I really trust a guy who has a crown in his bedroom?

Especially one who only seems to be awkward around ME?

I find an empty bench away from Georg and all his fantabulous friends and start rummaging through my backpack, trying to ignore the horrible pressure in my chest that tells me I am falling for the wrong guy. Again. I shove my wallet out of the way and find a half-smashed tampon—of course, a day late—then realize that I still need that tampon. I only have four left at home.

Crap.

I'm going to have to stop at that quickie mart on the way home and hope they stock girly products with English labels or some kind of picture, so I don't accidentally buy Depends or something equally revolting. I also have to hope that Georg and his friends aren't stopping into the store for the Schwerinborg equivalent of Twizzlers.

I check my wallet to make sure I have enough cash, then realize I'm screwed. All I have is one euro—which is about the same as a buck—and an American twenty-dollar bill. Since the cafeteria takes a swipe card that deducts from Dad's bank account, I hadn't thought to ask him for any euros other than what I needed for the Coke machine in the Munich airport.

This is bad. Very bad. And I so don't want to ask Dad to buy me tampons. That'd just be wrong.

"Hi. It's Valerie, isn't it?"

I bury the tampon under a couple of books in my backpack and smile at the feminine voice to my left. The quad's pretty crowded, but there are three girls looking at me. I think the blond one spoke—I introduced myself to her in chemistry yesterday. "Hi. Yeah, it's Valerie. You're Ulrike, right?"

She nods, and the look on her face isn't openly hostile or anything, so I figure I'm okay. Ulrike is one of those girls I'm always suspicious of based on looks alone, though Christie tells me this is really shallow. Ulrike's about five-foot-seven, and has this white-blond hair that looks shimmery, even today with the misty weather and nothing but the gray high school building and the snowy Alps behind her. In the sunshine, you just know she's stunning.

"I heard you live at the palace?" she says, still smiling at me.

"Yeah, my dad works for Prince Manfred."

"So you must know Georg?" Another one of the girls jumps in without bothering to introduce herself. She's a teeny tiny brunette, and totally pretty. Of course.

"We've talked a couple times." I drop my backpack onto the bench beside me and make a point not to look across the quad toward Georg. I'm not sure why, but all of a sudden my bullshit detector's blaring, and it's warning me to keep things chill. "But I just moved here a couple weeks ago, so I really don't know anyone yet."

"Well, now you know us," Ulrike smiles, though the girl who asked if I know Georg doesn't seem all that thrilled about Ulrike talking to me.

They—well, mostly Ulrike—invite me to eat lunch with them, so I do, even though it's more like they're eating with me, since I was the one who snagged the bench in the first place. I wonder if I'm in their spot or something.

Ulrike's okay, I decide after a few minutes. Just from listening to her talk, I can tell she's fairly popular. She's into sports and apparently she's on student council. Her dad's some kind of diplomat from Germany. The third girl, Maya, moved here from New York when she was six for her mom's international banking job. She's a junior, but she and Ulrike live next door to each other and play soccer together, so they hang out a lot.

I keep glancing at the brunette who asked me about Georg, hoping she'll introduce herself. Ulrike finally does it for her: Her name's Steffi, and of course Ulrike says all kinds of nice things about her, including the fact that Steffi's vice president of the sophomore class—excuse me, of *year ten*—and was elected to homecoming court last year *and* this year. I tell Steffi I'm glad to meet her (hey, Dad raised me to be well mannered) and that it's cool she's on student council with Ulrike. Of course, the whole time Steffi just sits there eating her tuna on wheat like what Ulrike's saying is no big thing. Then, when I compliment Steffi on this funky hair clip she's wearing, she only shrugs. Not an embarrassed-to-becomplimented shrug, but a shrug that makes it clear she thinks she's entitled to a compliment or two.

I hate her already.

Finally the warning bell rings. I wad up my trash and Steffi does the same. Then she hesitates and looks up. I think she's actually going to speak to me.

Not.

"Hey, Georg," she says with a megawatt grin plastered all over her face. I turn around, and of course there he is. He's intentionally not looking at me as he gives us a group hello.

Do I have a big, fat letter *L* stamped on my forehead, or what?

Georg asks Maya how much homework got assigned in French IV today, since he's heading there next. While Maya flips through a blue notebook looking for the assignment, I start to tell Georg what it is, since I had French IV with the same teacher right before lunch.

This is the moment Steffi finally deigns to speak to me. "Oh, Valerie," she says in this repellent whisper that's totally meant to be heard, "did you ever solve your little problem yesterday? I saw you headed into the first-floor bathroom after school, and you looked desperate!"

I want to smack her. She is evil, evil, evil. And was she freakin' *following* me or something?

Georg swallows and looks uncomfortable, though his eyes are totally focused on Maya, which means he heard Steffi but is pretending he didn't. When Maya finally finds the right page in her notebook and tells him the assignment, he scribbles it down, then heads to class, with Steffi right at his elbow, because of course her Spanish III class is right next door to French IV.

He doesn't even look at me.

And naturally Steffi never notices that I didn't answer her. Bitch.

The whole way home—I take the *strassenbahn* again, just because I know Georg is still in the school building and can't cross the quad fast enough to jump on the same one—I'm thinking I should e-mail Jules and tell her that to date, my Armor Girl theory is dead on. It's even correct on an international scale, because I am beginning to suspect that Steffi is going to play the role of Shallow Princess to my Armor Girl.

Here's the evidence:

1) Georg liked talking to me over break, but no one else was around. This clearly makes me a "safety" girl, like the Armor Girl—someone who makes you smile during those trying times when there are no Shallow Princesses around to kiss up to you.

2) I drew a flattering picture of Georg. Armor Girl made Heath some cool armor. Both of us do nice things without expecting anything in return.

3) In public, the hero walks off with the Shallow Princess and totally forgets about the Armor Girl.

I try think of a number four, but I can't. Truth is, when I push the analogy, it doesn't work.

Heath never kissed the Armor Girl and gave her the let's-be-friends speech. He never acted like he liked her that way at all. Maybe that part of the movie ended up on the cutting-room floor, I don't know. But my gut tells me—despite what happened at lunch today, and despite the fact Georg didn't walk to school with me—that he really is a nice guy. He can't possibly be the type who would kiss an Armor Girl and forget all about it.

And it's not like he told me he's into Shallow Princess Steffi. Heath told Armor Girl flat out that he wanted the Shallow Princess, and he wanted her bad. He even had Armor Girl help him *get* Shallow Princess, and Armor Girl cheered when Heath kissed her. I even think she meant it.

If I saw Georg kiss Steffi, I'd hurl.

Okay, I am thinking about all this way, way too much.

And I'm getting tempted to call Mom and tell her I want to come live with her. Gabrielle, Lake Braddock, tofu dinners, and all.

When I get back to our apartment, Dad's already there. It's only three-thirty and he's supposed to be working, so I give him a little grin, even though I feel less than cheerful.

"Now that's not a happy smile." He stops messing around in the kitchen and frowns at me. "Bad day at school?"

Geez, is every thought I have that obvious?

"Nah." I drop my backpack onto the table, then open the fridge and grab a Coke Light. "Nothing some caffeine and a bowl of chocolate ice cream can't fix."

Dad reaches past me and puts his hand on the freezer door to hold it shut. "I promised your mother that you'd eat healthy foods. I picked up some fresh tilapia fillets this morning, and I'll make some vegetables to go with it. Get a few vitamins into your diet."

"Just give me a carrot to go with my ice cream," I retort, picking up a minicarrot from the pile of veggies he's already chopped into a bowl on the counter. He shakes his head, but moves away from the freezer and starts slicing an oversize yellow squash.

I take a sip of soda, then grab another carrot. "Besides, how's Mom going to know what I'm eating?"

"Maybe when you write her back?"

I freeze with the carrot halfway to my mouth. "Mom wrote me? A letter?"

He tips his head toward the Formica table. "It's under the Wal-Mart circular."

"Why did she send a Wal-Mart circular?"

"She didn't. It came in the regular mail."

"They have *Wal-Mart* in *Schwerinborg*?"

"They're everywhere." He laughs to himself as he covers the bowl of veggies with plastic wrap. "So if there's anything you need, remind me and we'll go this weekend. But I'll warn you, their products aren't quite like what you'd find at home. They carry mostly European brand names."

I flip past the Wal-Mart ad—despite Dad's offer to go shopping, I have zero interest in taking him shopping for feminine products, which is all I need, since he got me a new pillow and a hair dryer already—and see a large, padded manila envelope plastered with U.S. stamps. Mom's neat, rounded handwriting across the front gives me an instant wave of homesickness, as if I wasn't missing Virginia enough after the little episode with Steffi and Georg on the quad today.

"The fish needs to marinate," Dad says as he slides the veggies into the fridge, ready to sauté later. "I'm going to run out to handle a few things for Prince Manfred, so why don't we meet back here at five thirty for dinner?"

Did I mention how cool my dad can be? You'd think he'd be acting like Jules's mom did when her parents got divorced, asking Jules every five seconds what her father said about her. But even though I know he's curious (otherwise, how would he remember exactly where in the stack of mail he'd placed Mom's letter?) Dad's clearly going to give me some space.

I tell him that'll be fine, and once he's out the door, I rip the envelope open. A flat package, wrapped in pink paper with a silver ribbon, falls out onto the table. I resist the urge to tear into it and read the letter first, because I know Mom would want me to.

Dear Valerie,

I hope you're getting settled. I hate that you're so far away! I think about you every day, you know. I miss my baby girl.

Here, I'm getting moved into my new apartment. I'm also getting ready to look for a job. I don't have to do too much to get my teaching certification updated, so I'll soon be interviewing for elementary school positions for the fall. Wish me luck!

Gabrielle has agreed to be a leader for Weight Watchers and she's going through training now, which means that I'm alone at home a lot of nights. So if you're up late, you can call me anytime—you won't be bothering Gabrielle. And if you're feeling uncomfortable there, or school isn't going as you hoped, you know you always have a place to live with me. In the meantime, if you have a rough day, I've tucked in a little gift I hope will help you through.

I guess that's about it. I'm scheduled to get my Internet hookup next week, so I'll start e-mailing then. By the time you get this, I may be online, so check your computer!

Until then, please know that I'm thinking of you and your dad. I want you both to be happy, despite what you may think.

Lots and lots of love,
Mom

I put the letter down, then flop into the wobbly chair. I can't decide whether to open the gift or to peruse the Wal-Mart circular while I clear my brain.

I feel tears coming, but I grind my fists against my eye sockets for a minute to force them back. I'm not sure if I'm mad or depressed or what. All I know is that my life is royally jacked, and there's not a gift in the world short of a time machine that can fix it. And I'm not sure even that will help, since Mom seems to think she should have come out of the closet ten years ago. If I traveled back much farther than that to try to fix things, I wouldn't even have been born.

It's the kind of thing that only Captain Kirk or Jean Luc Picard would know how to fix. I don't belong here. Mom doesn't belong with Gabrielle, and she definitely shouldn't be teaching a bunch of elementary school kids. She taught fifth grade before she married Dad, but she swore up and down she'd never do it again. She said it drove her insane.

She obviously thinks insanity is preferable to being married to Dad.

I reread the letter, trying to convince

myself that Mom really does love me, and that on the inside she's the same person who took me to the beauty salon before homecoming and picked out the OPI Chick Flick Cherry nail polish for Christie and the Wyatt Earple Purple for me. Finally I slide it back into the envelope and open the gift. I'm not expecting much, but because it's the first really heartfelt gesture Mom's made since moving out, I figure it's worth a look.

And then I decide it's not. I missed my guess with Dad and the Chicken Soup book. Instead it's Mom with a book telling me not to sweat the small stuff.

She thinks my problems constitute *small stuff*?? On which freakin' planet, exactly, was she spawned?

Still, I open the book and flip to a random page in the back, which tells me I'm supposed to notice when my parents are doing things right. O-kay. Well, there's Dad and the fact he wants me to eat healthy, and he wants me to be happy. That's good.

I turn toward the front of the book, because I can't come up with anything about Mom. She says she wants me to be happy, but . . .

Maybe if I start closer to the beginning of the book I can work my way up to appreciating Mom.

As I go back to chapter 1, a page in the middle catches my eye. I stop and read about the importance of creating my own special space.

I look around the apartment. Ugly furniture and a bad view cannot possibly be the criteria needed for a special space.

Without thinking about it, I take the book and the envelope and head for the library.

Eight

My special place turns out to be not-so-special. Or at least, not special in the sense that I'm the only one who gets to hang out here. Because, wouldn't you know, within ten minutes of me flopping in the chair and burrowing way down—mostly so Karl can't see me from the hallway and decide to come in and offer me pretzels—Georg walks right up to the chair to see if I'm in it.

And he says he's been looking for me.

He starts to sit in the chair beside me, clearly not taking the hint that I'm scrunched up all small into this honking big chair because I want to be alone. But then he sees my not-so-welcoming face and hesitates. My face is hot from crying so I'm willing to bet it looks all blotchy and red—which is pretty scary.

"Hey, you've been crying."

Duh. "Oh, no," I lie. Why not, now that I'm getting in the habit? "It's just allergies."

"Of course. Everyone has bad allergy problems in January." He frowns, then looks down at the letter in my hand. "So what's that?"

I give him the Valerie Shrug. Okay, so I've been crying. I know I'm not a good liar. But I figure it might give him a clue. Apparently not.

"Look," I tell him, "you know how you hate that people treat you differently because you're a prince? They see the castle or your expensive clothes and make certain assumptions?" Or so he says—about hating the attention, that is. It's totally obvious at school that people treat him differently.

"Yeah?"

"Well, people aren't always what you see."

"Meaning?"

"Just because I've been crying doesn't mean I'm trying to get your attention. A lot of girls pull that crap, and if you want to know the honest truth, it pisses me off. So what you see isn't what you think it is. You don't need to hang out in here because you think I need some attention. I'm just fine all by myself."

He shoves his hands into the front pockets of his Levi's and leans forward, so his chest is against the back of the empty chair. The expression on his face goes flat, then he looks right into my eyes, and I know before he says a word that I've gone too far.

"And just because I came in here to ask what happened doesn't mean I think that you're trying to get my attention. And if you want to know the honest truth"—his mouth curls up at the edges as he parrots my words—"I thought things sucked at lunch today, so I wanted to come down here and talk to you about what happened and apologize."

"You didn't bother trying to talk to me about it at school. You saw me standing by my locker after last period." Not when all his friends were around. Why be nice to the new girl?

"You didn't look like you wanted to be bothered. I assume this all has something to do with yesterday, when we were hanging out in the balcony, which is another reason I didn't bring it up at school. It's nobody else's business."

Okay, I'll give him that. I did turn away from him and his snobby-looking clique to find my own bench when we were on the quad today, though he looked away from me first.

But the *real* truth is that my current runny-nose-scuzzy-crying-face isn't even about him.

"Well, you're right when you say school was rotten today." I try not to sniffle, and wish I'd been smart enough to tuck a tissue in my pocket. "But I'm dealing with some other stuff and that's why I'm all whacked out right now. It's nothing major or anything, I just have to get past being hyper about the small stuff."

Okay, so I did start reading the book from Mom. And now I'm trying to convince myself that in the grand scheme of life, my parents getting a divorce *is* small stuff. I mean, look at Jules's parents. They got divorced when we were all third graders—well, her mom got divorced a second time after that to remarry Jules's dad—but it all seems like it happened eons ago. Jules is still the same Jules she was before. A little more sarcastic, maybe, but we all knew by the end of our first play date that Jules was going to grow up with a major mouth. That's just how she's wired.

Third grade was exactly seven years ago. So I figure that by the time I'm legal drinking age, this won't be a big deal. It'll seem just as distant as Jules's parents' divorce. Small stuff, right?

I mean, I'm only in a library in a freakin' royal palace thousands and thousands of miles from the three best friends I've ever had, I've lost out on possibly becoming the girlfriend of a guy I've been mad about from the moment I first laid eyes on him in kindergarten when we were put in charge of feeding the class rabbit together, and my mother is living with a vegan blond weirdo who attributes her entire life philosophy to Weight Watchers.

Small stuff. Little itty bitty infinitesimal tiny stuff.

Georg comes around and sits in the chair beside mine, though he's moving slowly, like he thinks I'll fling myself at him in a jealous-over-Steffi rage at any moment for ignoring me at lunch. Or maybe he's worried I'll emotionally vomit all over him because I'm just having such a horrid day. (This is a no-no according to the very first page of the small stuff book. It says you shouldn't vomit all over your friends by taking every ounce of your messed-up emotions and dumping them in your friends' laps. I can relate, since I'm usually the one on the receiving end of such vomit.)

"Is the letter from your mom?"

I nod. I'm too worn out to dodge him. And you know, those intense Colin Farrell–like gazes of his are getting to me.

"My dad told me your parents are in the middle of a divorce." He shifts in his chair, and it's obvious he's not comfortable talking about this, but he's making the effort.

"Did your dad tell you why?"

He nods.

"Well, then you know everything."

"You mad at your mom?" He nods toward the letter again.

I am not going to commit emotional vomit. I'm not.

"A little," I say. "I mean, I'm the teenager and she's the adult. I'm the one who's supposed to be figuring out what I want in life, not her. She had it all. And the whole thing just makes me mad at myself."

Georg is kind enough not to agree. "At yourself? What'd you do?"

"I'm just being shallow about it, is all. I need to get over it. I'm just not getting over it as fast as I should, and that's pissing me off."

"I think it'd be hard for anyone to handle, so I don't see how you're being shallow."

"Well, first, I'm not trusting my mom as much as I should. We've always been really tight, and it's hard for me now."

"That's understandable."

"Yeah, but it's shallow. I should be more supportive, but I'm not. I just totally react against it. Like, how about this: Sometimes when I look at you, I think *Gay*-org, instead of *Georg,* and it automatically gives me the willies?"

He puffs out a breath in surprise. "Wow. That's bad."

"I'm saying. I'm being shallow about it, and it's pissing me off that I'm acting this way."

Okay, I cannot believe I just blurted out the whole Gay-org thing. I mean, despite what I just said, it hasn't occurred to me since the first day I met him. I've gotten used to Georg being Georg. His name doesn't sound weird to me anymore.

It actually sounds kind of sexy and exotic. Of course, that could just be his accent affecting me.

Maybe I told him because I felt guilty.

"So take it one step at a time," he says. "If Georg bugs you so much—which I totally get—you can just call me Jack. My middle name is Jacques, after my French grandfather."

I'm stunned. I know I'm about as shallow as a person can be, but I didn't want *him* to do anything about it. Like tell me to call him something else. This is my problem.

"I'm *not* going to call you Jack," I tell him. "That'd just be wrong."

He holds up his hands as if to say, *Whatever.*

"Look, I really appreciate it. But I'll call you Georg. And I'll eventually get over the whole thing. Honestly, Georg is a perfectly cool name. And I'm not really *that* shallow." At least, I hope I'm not. I never thought so before.

"And I'm not either," he says, his voice dead serious.

I set Mom's letter facedown on the end table and frown. "You think I think you're shallow?"

"Well, I was an ass today at school. I saw you leaving this morning and walked ahead. And then I tried not to look at you at lunch."

"Why?"

He screws up his mouth in this way that's totally cute, despite the fact I so *don't* want to find him cute right now. "I don't know. Maybe because I can't help but spend all my time worrying about what everyone thinks. I don't want to make anyone angry, and if I show the slightest interest in you, people will start with the gossip, and someone's bound to get ticked off. It's been this way since I was a little kid, and I'm not getting any better at it. I try to be nice to everyone, but because I'm a prince, people think they know me. And they all want something from me. If I don't give it to them, then they do things like Steffi did today."

"So you did hear her." I mock Steffi's drama queen fakey whisper as I say it.

"Who didn't? Word of warning—" His eyes sharpen for a split second. "I can be honest here, right?"

"You can with me. I don't want anything from you." Well, maybe I do, if we're being honest here. But I'd want it whether or not he was a prince.

"Steffi's a bitch. Ulrike and Maya are all right, for the most part, but watch out for Steffi. It sounds like I'm on a total ego trip to say so, but she kind of has a thing for me."

Wow. Georg called someone a bitch and did it with perfect posture. He really is getting relaxed around me. And of course, this is driving me insane.

I mean, how do I get over it? He's beyond out of my league. And he said flat-out he wanted to be my friend. Nothing else.

"What she did to you today is typical,"

Georg explains. "I was hoping that if I acted like you didn't exist, she wouldn't think we knew each other and wouldn't pay any attention to you. As nasty as that sounds, trust me, with her it's better not to exist." He looks apologetic as he adds, "But I shouldn't have ignored you. I mean, I might have deflected Steffi a little, but it was still wrong. I'm sorry."

I manage to keep from grinning at his totally whacked pronunciation of *deflected,* and tell him apology accepted, but totally unnecessary.

Which is a lie, too, because I'm glad he apologized.

He kicks his foot out and toys with the leg of my chair. "Look, you're worried about what people will think of you because of your mom. Which is why you never said anything to me about her, right?"

I swallow hard. Damn, but he just cuts to the guts of it. "I never even told my friends in Virginia. I only told them my parents were getting a divorce. No details."

"What if I told you I understand because I do the same thing every single day?"

I just raise my eyebrows. I mean, come on. His parents are about as perfect as you get.

"Did you see the guy in the black leather jacket walking between you and me on the sidewalk this morning? He was carrying coffee, looked like he was headed to work?"

I think for a minute, then nod. "Blond guy."

"He works for *Majesty* magazine. He follows me at least once a week. Usually more."

I can't even respond. I mean, geez! No wonder Georg was acting all bizarro and looking over his shoulder while he walked. It didn't have anything to do with me at all.

"I fake my way through school just so I can avoid dealing with people like Steffi, then I hide out at home," he explains, and he just looks more and more frustrated as he talks. "But when I'm home, I'm not completely happy either. I've got my dad on my case about my responsibility to get good grades and to be more mature than most kids my age, because otherwise no one will have faith in me as a leader. And my dad's always showing me tabloid articles about him, or about my mom, and telling me how the slightest thing can get taken the wrong way, so I need to be on my guard all the time."

He looks so serious, and his face is so caring, I believe him. I really do.

"So I guess it's not just a life of going to polo parties or getting any girl you want, huh?"

He snorts. "I've never ridden a horse in my life. And if I did, I'd probably fall off, and the whole world would get it in full color in the tabloids or in one of those royalty magazines. Can't you just see it, a big picture of me with mud and horse manure all over my face?"

"Ouch," I say. Guess I never realized before that he would so get the whole who-my-parents-are-is-ruining-my-life thing.

"And," he adds, leaning forward a little. "I don't get any girl I want."

I roll my eyes and laugh. "Okay, you had me with your life-isn't-always-fun-for-a-prince shtick, but I have to tell you, I don't believe the girl part of it. You're lucky they don't rip your designer clothes right off your body in the middle of the quad."

He cocks his head sideways. "Would *you* go out with me, after the way I treated you at school today? Or what happened in the balcony yesterday?"

I'm about to make a sarcastic reply—I can't help it, it's what I do—but then I realize he's serious. *Completely* serious.

How did *that* happen? Especially when I look like absolute hell?!

"Let's make a deal. You talk to your mom, get your feelings out on the table, try to give her a break," he says. "I think it'll make you feel better, because in your gut, it's what you really want to do. It's what you'd do if you weren't worrying about what everyone will think."

I'm about to protest, but he says, "And I'll do the same. You get honest with your mom, and I'll be honest with you. I'd rather not be just friends."

I think I'm going to hurl. In a good way though. I mean, he just made my stomach do the best kind of twist.

Whoa.

He scoots forward in his chair, and he's sitting so close I can reach out and touch him and make it look like a total accident if I want.

"Meaning?" I don't think I can breathe waiting for him to say something.

"Meaning I kind of freaked out yesterday when we got to the balcony. I was afraid maybe I offended you or I moved too fast . . . I don't know. I didn't even really plan to kiss you yesterday, I just did. And then, after having such a cool afternoon with you, I was a total ass this morning. I got all hung up on the reporter and Steffi—I just did what I wanted and kind of forgot everyone else. Including you." He does that funky raising-one-eyebrow thing. "So you see, you're not the only one who's shallow."

"I guess that's a good thing," I say, and even though it all seems surreal, I want him to kiss me again. Especially since yesterday I screwed up kissing him back. Maybe this time I'll get it right.

His foot bumps against mine, and he doesn't pull it back. "So does that mean you'd consider going out with me? Since we're both so shallow and everything?"

"As long as we don't double with Steffi." I know. I know. I can't be serious even when it's important. Christie tells me not to get goofy when I'm nervous, but I do anyway. I'm going to have to work on that.

Later, though, because Georg actually laughs at that one.

"Well, I have this thing to go to tomorrow night. I know it's last minute to ask, but I was hoping my parents wouldn't make me go."

"It sounds like fun already," I tease him.

"Well, I thought it might be if you come. It's this dinner and dancing thing. It's in the reception hall—the room below where we were in the balcony. There's a summit on global warming tomorrow in Zurich, and the British prime minister is going to be there. Afterward he's coming here to meet with my dad. So they're doing a banquet dinner, and then there's going to be a ball before the P.M. flies back to London in the morning."

As he's describing who's coming and what the whole evening's about, I start getting concerned that my eyes might pop right out of my skull. This is way, way out of my league. It's totally my dad's kind of thing.

Geez, he's probably coaching staff members on what to say and do at this exact moment.

"So?" he asks.

I take a deep breath. "Well, I was kind of expecting you to ask if I wanted to go to McDonald's or catch a movie. Having dinner with a prime minister—not to mention *your parents*—is kind of a big first date."

I hope I don't sound like I'm dissing him, because I'm actually as psyched about this as I am scared to death. "And my dad is probably going to be there too. Wouldn't that be kind of weird?"

"Maybe we can sneak out after dinner, then."

I can't help but smile at him. "We'd probably get in trouble."

"Nah. I'd just say I was showing you the way to the ladies' room or giving you a palace tour or something."

"I've already had a palace tour."

The grin on his face is downright wicked. "So I offered and you thought it would be rude not to accept."

This is so going to get me in trouble, but I could just eat this guy alive. I love that he wants to do something risky, and that he wants me to do it with him. "Okay. Then I accept."

I smile, and inside, I hope he's going to kiss me, because he's smiling too, as big as if he just kicked the winning goal in the final two seconds of a championship soccer match. But no. He starts talking about when and where we can meet up before-hand, then he ducks out of the library so he won't be late to dinner.

When I'm alone again, I pick up the book and the letter from my mom to take them back to the apartment. I hope I don't look too blotchy, or Dad's going to think that Mom's letter really messed me up. I sit down for a second to get my head on straight, and suddenly I realize that what I thought was my special place might be *our* special place. Mine and Georg's.

And I'm completely cool with that.

To: Val@realmail.sg.com
From: ChristieT@viennawest.edu
Subject: CALL!!

Val,

You are NOT going to believe this. Natalie got her TONGUE PIERCED yesterday!!! She didn't tell us or even take any of us with her. Can you believe it?

Anyway, my mom said I can call you tomorrow night! Will you be there? It would be right after school for me, about nine at night for you. Let me know. I have all kinds of good dirt for you. Trust me, it's important stuff that you MUST hear, and it has nothing to do with my cousins' visit.

I just couldn't wait to tell you about Natalie, though. Her parents haven't seen it yet (though the way she's moaning and groaning about how it hurts and not eating, you'd think they'd notice).

If they grounded her for a week for Girl Scouts, you just know she's in for it big-time now. I'll let you know what happens. Cannot WAIT to talk to you! Big, big news.

Love, Christie :)

To: ChristieT@viennawest.edu
From: Val@realmail.sg.com

Subject: RE: CALL!!

Christie,

AACK!! You are going to kill me twelve times over. I won't be here tomorrow night!! Any chance you can call tonight (if you get this in time) or day after tomorrow?

I'm DYING to talk to you, and I have a lot of dirt too. You're not going to believe it. Seriously, this is more unbelievable than Natalie's piercing or whatever else it is you have to tell me.

I miss you!!

Val

PS—You do know that Natalie has a tattoo already, right? If you didn't already know, though, I didn't tell you. She has a little heart by her shoulder blade. Her parents DEFI-NITELY haven't seen it. That's why she "for-got" to pack a swimsuit when her family went to Florida last year.

PPS—I DID NOT TELL YOU, get it?! Pretend to see it yourself next time she's trying on clothes at your place.

To: Val@realmail.sg.com
From: CoolJule@viennawest.edu
Subject: Are you INSANE?

Val,

What do you mean, I beat up my brother all the time even though his name is Mike, which is normal?

It's so not normal. Think about it.

Okay . . . did you think about it?

His name is MICHAEL JACKSON, you freak.

So yes, I would have beat up Manfred for his name. Please. Give me some credit.

Jules

PS—When are you going to write to me about something important? Like that hottie you live with and what he said when you gave him my phone number?

I am going on a date with Georg.

I am going on a date with Georg Jacques von Ederhollern of Schwerinborg.

I am going on a date with the guy who

has the strangest name in the world and I'm completely and totally okay with that, because I'm learning not to sweat the small stuff.

I am going on a date with a guy who is laid back and easy to talk to and who can see through people like Steffi the same way I can.

I am going on a date with A FREAKIN' PRINCE!! TOMORROW!!

This is too much. I have to tell Christie about it. About EVERYTHING. I mean, who has their first date with the British prime minister at the table?!

Since with the time difference I know Christie's still at school, I flop in the living room after dinner, half watching a German-dubbed John Wayne movie, half freaking out over how strange my life has become.

And then I tell Dad.

I have to. I mean, he's in charge of protocol. You think he wouldn't find out I have a date with Georg?

He is currently sitting next to me on our not-so-comfy couch trying to absorb it all, and muttering to himself about all the stuff he wishes he'd thought to teach me about proper decorum. I keep telling him it's not a *real* date, even though in my gut I know it is.

That's what makes it so incredible.

"Look"—I turn to Dad and keep my voice as light and sincere as possible—"I talked to Georg about the whole thing, and he says that there's no receiving line. I can meet his parents beforehand, so it's nothing major, and at the dinner itself I don't have to talk to anyone other than him if I don't want to. So I can just lie low, okay?"

Dad picks up the remote and clicks off *X-Men,* the movie that's now starting on TV, then presses his fingers to his temples. I want to say more—to explain that I won't embarrass him, or that I didn't keep hanging out with Georg on purpose so we could hook up—but I don't think anything I say is going to make Dad any less worried.

I mean, *X-Men* is one of his favorite movies. He wouldn't shut it off unless he was really concerned.

"Valerie"—he finally sits up straight and turns toward me—"is this something that's really important to you?"

I stare at him for a sec, trying to figure out just what he's asking. "Why? Is this going to make you lose your job?"

He goes from serious to laughing in a nanosecond. "No. Well, unless you do something truly horrific, like start a food fight with Prince Manfred or insult Princess Claudia's taste in clothes in front of a reporter. You're not planning to do that, are you?"

"Um, *no*."

"So you like Georg, I take it?"

Well, duh. "I think he's really nice, Dad. And you said just a few days ago that you think he has a good reputation."

"That's true." He leans back against the arm of the couch and crosses his arms over his chest. "So you can go. But on one condition."

I gesture for him to get on with it, even though I'm dreading the condition. Dad never gives good conditions. It's always, you can go out, but you can't stay out after nine—in other words, late enough to have any fun. And I'm planning on having a lot of fun with Georg.

A *lot*. I'm due.

"I get to play fairy godmother. So to

speak. Help you pick a dress, coach you a little on what to say to Prince Manfred and Princess Claudia."

The idea of my totally buffed-up Dad picking out a dress with me is hysterical. His clothes always look perfect, and totally stylish, so maybe it'll be a bonding experience. And I can always veto his choice if he wants something butt ugly. I hope.

"Okay. But we don't have much time to shop," I tell him.

"Then let's go now." He jumps off the couch and pockets his wallet before I can even say anything. "I've heard Princess Claudia mention a few places that should still be open. But we'll have to hurry. The stores here don't stay open nearly as late as they do in the States."

I follow him out the door, and I have to admit I'm not nearly as freaked as I was before I told Dad about the date.

And, you know, I didn't even make one joke about Dad using the term *fairy god-mother* in reference to himself, which is very tempting given the whole gay Mom thing. I must be learning.

Christie would be proud.

Nine

To: BarbnGabby@mailmagic.com
From: Val@realmail.sg.com
Subject: Everything

Hi, Mom!

Dad said you called last night and gave him your new e-mail address. Is this an address for both you and Gabrielle, or just you? (I can't really tell from your BarbnGabby handle.)

Anyway, Dad also said he told you about my date tonight. Thanks for being so excited for me. He even helped me find a fantastic dress. Can you believe it? I promise to send you another e-mail tomorrow to tell you how the whole thing tonight goes.

Also, your package arrived yesterday. I know I make fun of you a lot because you buy so many self-help books, (especially the one about somebody moving your cheese—I'm still not sure I get that one) but it was nice of you to send me the small stuff book. It's really good, and no, that doesn't mean you should buy me more books to balance me emotionally. One is enough, and I am now balanced.

Thank you.

I hope you're happy in your new apartment and that you're excited about teaching school again, though I will say it kind of surprises me. I didn't think you liked it that much. I thought you'd do something else if you went back to work.

I'll write again tomorrow.

Love,
Valerie

Go figure. Dad has really, *really* good taste in dresses. And he's clearly been saving money—now that he's not bringing home little gifts for Mom all the time, I suppose—because he let his credit card take a mighty hit yesterday without flinching. This never, and I mean *never,* happens. I don't even get an allowance. All my money comes from baby-sitting. Well, all my money *came* from baby-sitting. Eventually, I'm going to have to learn enough German to get a job at the Schwerinborg McDonald's or something.

Not that I can think about that right now.

I just hope Mom doesn't find out how much he spent, though maybe she won't care anymore. I mean, she and Dad finally agreed on a lump sum for alimony without having to deal with lawyers, and I know it's plenty, even though he doesn't have to give her any child support or anything.

But I am determined not to hold against her the fact she kept telling Dad (usually with Gabrielle in the room) that he could afford to pay her a hell of a lot more. Really.

Small stuff, right?

I take a deep breath—doing my best to think only good thoughts about Mom or nothing at all, because if I let myself, I could go on all day about her stupid choice of an e-mail address, let alone the money thing—and I turn back around to face the full-length mirror that Dad was brilliant enough to have installed on the back of the door to my bathroom. The bathroom's so tiny I have to stand in the shower to see all of me in the mirror, but it doesn't matter.

I look totally hot.

I've always hated my red hair. Not so much because it's different—that's the one thing I like about it—but because it makes me look not-quite-right in clothes and makeup.

Clothes have to stay basic—grays and blacks and stuff—or I could seriously blind someone. Contrary to popular belief and my mother's shopping tendencies, jewel-tone greens and blues do *not* look good on redheads. It makes us look like we belong on the cast of *Dynasty* or *Falcon Crest* or some other corny, over-the-top eighties TV drama. Just picture Nicole Kidman as a teenager in electric pink and you get the idea. *Hideous.* So I limit the colored shirts I wear to my one—*one*—red floral top that Christie bought me for Christmas last year at Express and a funky blue halter I got at Abercrombie & Fitch.

And while clothes can be a challenge, makeup is worse. The chemists at your big cosmetics companies design makeup in shades that look fantastic on your average brown- or blue-eyed, dirty-blond-to-brunette person. Those colors just don't work on someone whose face is so shockingly white that wearing reflective gear for an evening run through the neighborhood is redundant.

But Dad outdid himself here. I mean, our shopping trip was almost like an episode of E!'s *Fashion Emergency* come to life. Only I was the emergency and he was this hunky version of Leon Hall and had all the store clerks melting.

First, he got me this killer—and I mean *killer*—dress. As in, the thing is a deep, blood red. Beyond red. I never, ever would have pulled this thing off the rack, but Dad insisted I try it on, and even though I argued with him the whole way to the dressing room, trying to explain the whole butt-ugly-redhead-in-bright-colors concept, I took back every word the instant I got the thing over my head and got an eyeful in the store's three-way mirror.

It makes me look like a freaking *goddess.*

And the thing is, the other reason I wear a lot of black is because it lets me blend in and not look like I'm trying too hard to be noticed. This dress—believe it or not—does the same thing. It's classy and understated. And it's RED. Go figure!

I turn around in the shower for a final inspection. I'm being pretty harsh on myself as I look in the bathroom mirror, trying to see what I look like if I slouch, when I sit, or if I act flirty. But even if I *try* to look like a desperate girly-girl, which is pretty easy to do when you're standing in a circa 1970s shower stall, I don't.

In this dress, I actually look confident.

How did Dad do that?! It's like he's even *better* than Leon Hall. Maybe right up there with the hoity-toity hotel manager from *Pretty Woman* who knew just how to turn Julia Roberts from a total ho into Richard Gere's dream girl.

Now that I think of it, Julia's dress in that movie was red too. Freaky.

Anyway, the best part of the shopping trip came after the red dress, when Dad parked me at a cosmetics counter and told the ladies to go to work. He had them redo my face twice, since he didn't like what they did on the first *or* second go-round. Then he handed the woman behind the register his plastic and gave her a limit, telling her to get me the most essential items needed to re-create the look, while he headed off to the shoe department.

No, really. I'm not kidding. Dad picked out my *shoes.*

And you wonder why, if I'd had to peg one of my parents as having gay tendencies, Dad came to mind before Mom.

He brought me these totally fun strappy things to try on—they let him, because they could see me at the makeup counter from the shoe department, plus I think the shoe department lady thought my dad was cute—and even though the shoes were kind of sexy, they weren't so high they were uncomfortable.

It usually takes me trying on, like, ten pairs of heels to find a pair that fits and feels comfy. I'm much more the Skechers and Steve Madden shoe type than one of those girls who wears four-inch heels, and it's usually obvious when I actually *need* a pair of heels how unnatural they are on me. But Dad found the perfect pair on his first try. And now that I'm looking at the whole thing in the full-length mirror, I realize how awesome they look with the dress.

And that's standing in the shower. I cannot imagine how kickin' this is going to look once I'm in that big, fancy reception hall with chandeliers and candlelight.

I might actually look like a girl who is pretty enough to go to dinner with a prince.

When I finally walk out of the bathroom to show Dad, he's standing in the living room wearing his tux. He doesn't say anything. He just smiles.

You'd think I was wearing white and standing at the back of a church about to take his arm, he's so proud of himself.

He has to leave for dinner earlier than me, since he needs to be available to Prince Manfred as soon as the British prime minister arrives at the palace, but I know he's happy I got dressed an hour early, just so he could check me out before he has to leave.

All I can do is tell him thanks. And that I am so, so glad I decided to come with him to Schwerinborg, even if I did have to leave all my friends and my entire social life a couple thousand miles away. Because I know he loves me and wants to do whatever it takes for me to be happy—even when that means making me study an extra hour for a geometry exam so I can be proud of how I've done.

He shakes his head and laughs, but it's not an altogether happy laugh. I can tell he wants to give me another warning about Georg. He's totally worried that I'm getting into more than I can handle since Georg's not your typical guy, no matter how much I want to believe it.

Luckily, he knows I know that, and he leaves without saying anything.

I walk back to the bathroom and look in the mirror again, trying to see what Georg will see.

For the first time in my life, I *so* hope I'm going to get more than I can handle.

To: Val@realmail.sg.com
From: ChristieT@viennawest.edu
Subject: I CAN'T WAIT ANOTHER DAY!!!

Val,

Okay, first of all, I cannot BELIEVE you're not going to be home tonight. Second of all, I don't care WHAT you think your unbelievable news is, mine is unbelievable-er.

I got your e-mail too late yesterday to call then, because it would have been about 2 AM your time. So even though I wanted to tell you everything on the phone, I will give you a hint now.

David spilled his guts to Jeremy yesterday. And I mean SPILLED. And it was about YOU.

Is that enough of a hint about what I need to say to make you stay home so I can call you? Does this not make whatever it is you want to tell me suck in comparison?

I'll try calling tonight just in case, but if you're not there, I'll call again tomorrow night. You MUST hear all my gossip.

You said you could come home if things weren't good in Schwerinborg. I'm telling you, you should seriously consider COMING HOME! Now is most definitely the time.

Details during the phone call.

Love,
Christie, your very desperate, very pushy friend

I can't identify my soup, which is a light, minty green color. I also cannot identify the meat on my plate—some kind of fancy stuffed bird I have no idea how to eat. But I can't even think about the food, despite the fact food generally occupies a very high spot on my priority list.

Georg's leg is rubbing against mine under the table, and he's totally doing it on purpose.

And what's worse, I like it. A lot.

But what I cannot get over is that *David Anderson really likes me!* For *real.* After all these years. After all this wishing and hoping and fixing my hair just so and choosing at least one class I know he's going to be taking every quarter in the hope that he'll just *notice* me as something other than a friend. And now, apparently, he has. Or did.

That has to be what Christie wants to tell me. There just can't be another way to interpret her e-mail.

I think I am going to hurl all over the nice white tablecloth and fancy crystal goblets.

My stomach is just one big friggin' knot.

I wish, wish, WISH I'd just left to meet Georg in the library when Dad left the apartment. I could've found plenty of things to do while I was waiting. I could've sketched while I waited. I could've stared out the window. I could've relaxed in front of the fire with a nice leather-bound copy of Dickens or whatever it is Prince Manfred keeps on the library shelves.

Okay, so I'm not into Dickens.

But what I should *not* have done is go online to read my e-mail and make sure Christie got my message not to call tonight, because she just gave me way more information than I can handle.

What am I going to *do*?!?!

How is this even POSSIBLE?? How can TWO guys like me?

And how can I not know which one I really want?

No, I know which one I want. The one who actually talks to me about me and who gets the thing with my mom.

Right?

Then I feel Georg's fingers on my knee. I'm so surprised I bump against the table, even though he's had his leg touching mine the whole meal. He starts making little circles with his fingers, twisting the red fabric of my dress into little swirls against my leg.

Okay, forget David.

I so want to go find a room with Georg. I mean, could he be any hotter?! He's wearing a tux, but it doesn't look stupid on him, like on most guys when they're going to the prom. He looks like he wears one all the time. And the best part is that the dark jacket shows off his blue eyes and his high cheekbones, making him look even more interesting and mysterious.

I glance to my left, where he's sitting. His parents are at another table across the room, talking with the British prime minister and smiling for the press photographers— there are about a dozen or so of them crowded along the walls on that end of the room—so I don't think anyone saw me jump. We're stuck sitting with the losers. Okay, not really losers—I mean, they're all fairly important people—but the press isn't clamoring for snapshots of them like they are of Manfred and Claudia. Our table is filled with people like Prince Manfred's private secretary, the minister of the treasury, and a couple of foreign diplomats— one of whom, Georg mentions, is Ulrike's father—who only care about whether they'll get a few minutes' conversation with the P.M. after dinner, and a few random staff members like my dad. Though thankfully, he's three people around the table from me, so he doesn't have a good angle to see me.

The only fairly important person on this whole side of the room is Georg's uncle, Prince Klaus, who's at the table behind us, with his back toward Georg's. I guess Klaus is Manfred's younger brother.

Could you imagine growing up in a house where the kids are named *Klaus* and *Manfred*?

Well, I've now been in Schwerinborg long enough to find this absolutely believable. I've also been here long enough to realize that the family members who aren't in the direct line of succession—people like Georg's uncle—and other diplomats get about a tenth of the attention someone like Georg does in the press, so they kind of run in their own little worlds. And on nights where politics is the hot topic, like tonight, the only press who show up are from the supersnooty papers and political magazines—reporters who'd rather figure out what the British P.M. tells Manfred about the environment than the fact that Georg brought a date to the dinner.

Of course, this means all of the people on our loser side of the room are talking to each other about their own little lives, and unless they get to meet the P.M., they don't care about being here. It's all same-old, same-old party circuit to them.

And none of them are looking at me or Georg.

I put my napkin up to my mouth and hiss, "Hey, cut it out."

He sneaks a look at the photographers, then at his uncle. Without looking directly at me, he says, "You don't like it?"

And he moves his fingers another inch or two higher.

Oh. My. God.

"No." I blot an imaginary bit of food from my mouth and glance at Dad, making sure Georg follows my point. "I do. But . . ."

He smiles and takes his hand off my knee. He waits a half beat, then gets a hunk of asparagus on his fork before whispering, "Good."

We keep quiet for the rest of the meal, but I can still feel where his fingers were on my leg, playing with my dress. Georg told me in the library, before we came in to the dinner, that he'd told his parents it was a date. However, he says that if it comes up, his parents are going to tell the reporter types that I'm the daughter of a staff member, and they thought it would be nice for Georg to finally have company his own age at one of these events. Period.

His parents were very cool when I met them too. They sound like they're as laid back as Dad, once they get away from the cameras and stuff. So maybe sneaking away after dinner won't be such a bad thing.

And then I feel Georg playing with my dress again under the table.

Oh, this is going to be bad. In a very, very good way.

"That was beyond boring," Georg says in his completely sexy accent once we're clear of the ballroom and finally feel safe enough to stop running and start walking. "Thanks for getting me out of there."

"You're the one who gave me the idea," I grin at him, trying to catch my breath. Poor Georg had been cornered by two ancient diplomats, and they were not-so-subtly grilling him about what he planned to study in college when I interrupted, as innocently as I could, and told Georg that we needed to go if we were going to finish the "planned tour" in time for him to be back to say good night to the P.M.

Ha!

The diplomats bought it, and the second Georg and I were out the ballroom door, he told me to run—well, as fast as I could in my new heels—and I followed him until I was totally lost. Now that we're finally walking, I realize we're in the long hallway that leads out to the gardens behind the palace. I walked through here on my *real* palace tour the day Dad and I arrived. It's completely empty now, except for me and Georg. And the lights are all off, except for some hidden, faint lights near the floor. Totally romantic, even with the pictures of all the old, gruesome-looking men on the walls and the sour-faced statues scattered here and there beside the closed doors.

"Well, thanks a lot for interrupting when you did. I'm so sick of having all my parents' friends butt into my business, you can't even imagine." He looks angry as he adds, "They weren't asking about school and stuff to be friendly. It's that they think they have the right to tell me what to do, like they think I'm not following the correct path for Schwerinborg."

"Like you won't turn out to be as good a prince as your father if you don't take AP Physics next year?"

"Exactly."

"That blows."

This, of course, makes him laugh, which I think is what he really needs.

We walk along in silence for a while. It's a good silence, though, and Georg takes my hand like it's the most natural thing in the world to him.

And the really scary thing is that it feels totally natural to me, too. Exciting and majorly nerve-racking, but natural. Like we're *supposed* to be holding hands.

"Do you think they'll notice if we don't go back?" I ask as he leads me out an unguarded side door.

"Depends. My dad will be too busy to notice for hours. My mom might ask around though."

I almost ask him whether or not his mom will get mad, but the garden is so gorgeous, I quit caring.

"This rocks," I say, nodding toward an empty fountain a few feet in front of us. It's surrounded by benches, and you just know that it's full of staff in the summer, sitting and eating their lunches, listening to the water as it cascades down from the vase held by the goddess statue in the center. There's still snow in a few spots, but since today was warm, I'm guessing it'll be gone by tomorrow.

But somehow, the cold and the snow make the garden even more beautiful. Maybe because I know it'll be ours, all by ourselves.

"I come out here a lot," he says. "Especially in the winter. It's a lot nicer in the summer, but—"

"More crowded," we say at the same time, then we laugh.

Georg squeezes my hand, then pulls me a little closer. "You cold?"

I shake my head. I know it's the dead of winter, but I'm not, even in my wispy dress.

Then I realize what a dork I am—because of what he was really asking—and try to cover. "I mean, I wouldn't want to stay out all night, but it's not bad."

Georg slips off his jacket and slides it over my shoulders. I know it's totally corny, and so does he, but neither of us care.

"Better?"

I nod, and he takes my hand again, walking me a little farther from the back door, I think so no one sees us and starts gossiping.

"It's strange. I know we've only known each other a few weeks, but I feel like we *get* each other." He looks at me sideways, and I can't tell if he's being flirty or serious. "We're a lot alike."

I think so too, despite the fact that he's dark to my pale, every person in the world is dying to know the real Georg, (like anyone cares about the "real Valerie"), and he's got an accent that makes me want to jump all over him. But I never would have said what he did. I mean, it's fine for *him* to say it. But for me to say I'm a lot like a prince would come off as pretty damned egotistical.

"What?" he asks, misreading my silence.

"Nothing. It's just . . . I feel very comfortable with you too. This"—I wiggle my fingers in his hand—"this feels right. Cool, but scary at the same time, you think?"

"Like when I've got my hand on your leg under the table, with your father sitting right there?" He stops walking and faces me, and that wicked look is on his face again. We're behind a big hedge, so no one in the palace could see us if they tried, which is just *classic*. Even the air around us is cool and still, like it's waiting to see what happens next too.

Oh, I want him, bad.

"Especially then," I say. And I get bold, lean forward, and kiss him.

Because I can tell it's what we both want, but we're both too scared to start.

Ten

I know how to kiss. Go figure.

After all this time of stressing over whether or not I'd screw it up royally and make a complete and total fool of myself if a guy kissed me, and I mean REALLY kissed me, I find out that I can do it just fine, thankyouverymuch. Georg clearly has no clue this is the first time I've engaged in an intense makeout session. Again, thankyouverymuch.

And kissing Georg Jacques von Ederhollern is nothing like when Jason Barrows kissed me back in seventh grade. For one, Georg knows what he's doing. He is *good*. I mean, there's nothing sloppy or overeager about it. And he doesn't just kiss me with his mouth or his tongue.

I am learning in the best way possible that Georg is a full-body kisser.

Maybe it's supposed to be this way though—I mean, how would I know?

But what I *do* know is that when we hear voices in the garden—apparently one of the waiters and his girlfriend had the same thought we did—and scoot back into the palace, I want Georg to start from the beginning and kiss me all over again, because every single nerve ending in my whole body is doing this funky vibrating thing from wanting him. It's like someone stuck my finger in a socket and left my skin to sizzle.

Apparently Georg has the same thought, because his expression is totally intense as he pulls me along a couple of hallways without saying a word, then through another door.

When he flips on the light, though, every ounce of tension leaves my chest in a whoosh, and it's all I can do not to split my gut laughing.

"Oh, now *this* is totally romantic."

"You like the urinals?"

I laugh even harder, because I just can't help myself. He frowns. "That's the right word, isn't it?"

"Oh, yeah. They're urinals, all right."

"No one ever uses this restroom," he explains, pulling me past the two regular-size stalls and into the handicapped one on the end. I can hear the music thumping through the floor upstairs, and roll my eyes upward.

"The reception hall is right above us," he says as he wraps his arms around me, pulling me up against him again. "It has its own restrooms, though, so no one will bother us here."

"Good thing we managed to get outta there." I run my finger down his cheek. I love the way his skin feels. Smooth, but a different kind of smooth than mine. Like he shaved right before dinner. "I really prefer to dance to something besides whatever it is they're playing."

"It's Schubert."

"You a big Schubert fan?"

"Him and Eminem. Uncle Kracker would be okay too." He smiles and kisses me again, but gently this time, all soft and caring. My hip nearly bumps against the siderails of the stall, but he puts his hand there first, anticipating the collision.

"You hang out in these stalls often?" I tease. If he's brought other girls here though, I really don't want to know. I don't want anything to ruin tonight.

"Actually, this is the one place I can come to be alone. I've been hiding out in here since I was little. My parents have no clue."

He lets go of me and reaches behind the paper towel holder that's beside the handicapped stall's sink, half pulling the thing off the wall, and yanks out a pack of cigarettes.

I try to act cool, but I know I must look totally shocked.

"When I'm really, really having a bad day, I sneak down here and grab a smoke." He tosses the pack in the air, catches it with one hand, then tucks it back behind the holder and slams the metal cover back into place.

I'm so surprised I don't even know what to say. I thought Georg was Mr. Perfect. I mean, he plays soccer and gets awesome grades and doesn't even blast his music. Though I know the quiet music is because his parents want him to appear proper and all, I think he'd be smart and basically a clean-living guy without the pressure from his parents.

But he's just normal like me. I mean, *really* normal.

"I know you probably think it's disgusting," he says, but there isn't an apology in his voice. "But sometimes, I just need to do something—"

"Like in an emergency situation?"

"Yeah. I hate the smell on my clothes." The wicked grin returns, and he adds, "Plus my parents would kill me if they smelled it. I don't think they'd believe I smoke, but they'd be angry thinking I was even hanging out with anyone who smoked. God forbid some photographer snapped it."

"No kidding." I smile, just to let him know I don't think it's a big deal, and I totally wouldn't judge him for it.

I mean, he has no clue how relieved I am that he won't judge *me*.

I'm about to tell him that I've had a couple of emergency cigarettes too, and all about the Wendy's Dumpster and Jules and Natalie and Christie. I want to tell him I hate the smell and would never want to endanger my health, but that sometimes doing something dangerous or risky relieves all the pressure and stress at school—just like it took off all the pressure to do something risky tonight and sneak out of the reception—when the door opens so hard it whacks against the tile wall and sends the big letter *H* (which Georg tells me stands for *Herren,* the German word for "men") swinging on its screw.

Georg moves to shut the door to the handicapped stall, but it's too late. My dad has seen us.

Thankfully the tuxedoed man he's leading into the restroom hasn't. My dad eases the guy, who reeks like you wouldn't believe, into the next stall where he proceeds to worship the porcelain god very loudly.

My dad pulls the stall door shut behind the guy and says, "I'll be right here. Let me know if you want a towel."

The guy moans, then begins heaving again.

My dad isn't paying attention though. He's just glaring at me and Georg. Then his eyes drift past me to the floor, where the cigarettes have fallen from behind the paper towel holder onto the floor.

Oh, *shit*.

"I think you two need to head back to the ballroom," he says very quietly, though I doubt the guy on his knees in the next stall is in any shape to notice he and my dad aren't alone in here.

I want to tell my dad that we were *not* smoking. We weren't doing anything wrong. Not even hooking up—yet—but Georg just nods, then grabs my hand and pulls me behind my dad and out of the restroom.

"How much trouble are you in?" he whispers once we're out of there.

I shrug. "My dad's pretty cool. I doubt he'll rat you out to your parents."

Georg quirks his mouth, like it's no big thing. "I asked how much trouble *you* will be in."

"Truth? I don't know. But"—I feel the

same wicked grin Georg gives me spreading across my face—"I got busted last year with cigarettes. My parents know I don't smoke—it was an emergency situation thing—but they weren't exactly doing cartwheels. Getting caught twice could be bad."

"Wow. We really are alike," he says. He looks completely caught off guard by this, but in a good way. Like I just went up a notch in his mind, even though smoking isn't exactly a quality I want a guy to appreciate in me.

"You'll tell him we weren't smoking, right?"

"Of course," I say. "I'll tell him they were in the stall when we got there. He should know I'm telling the truth. It wasn't like one of us was standing there holding a lighter or the bathroom reeked."

"Not until the minister of the treasury showed up and gave back his quail."

The minister of the friggin' treasury? The guy who was sitting with us at dinner? I let out a little laugh, just to let Georg know I think everything will be okay. "If my dad can handle someone that important getting totally smashed, I bet he can handle seeing me in the men's room hanging with you."

"I suppose, if you explain it that way." Georg stops at the top of the stairs, pulling me over to the wall just before I turn the corner into the hall outside the ballroom. The Schubert morphs into Mozart—I think it's Mozart—but despite the fact the music is all classical, you can tell there's a serious party going on. The stairs are quiet compared to the boisterous chatter and clinking glasses of the ballroom.

"Before we go back"—he looks past me to make sure no one sees us, then back into my eyes—"I want you to know this has been one of the best nights of my life."

"Me too." I grin like a total goof, then take his tuxedo jacket off my shoulders and hand it back to him.

"I really like you, Valerie. A lot. I just—I mean—I want us to be together."

The knot in my throat is threatening to choke me, even more than the bird on my dinner plate did. "Thanks," I say, even though it's probably moronic to thank someone for liking you. "I really like you a

lot too. If you didn't notice out in the garden."

He grins at that, and our freaky-cool
connection feels stronger than ever. "So
would you like to dance with me? In front
of everybody?"

"Steffi will have a stroke."

"Steffi won't know." He's lying of
course, and we both know it, because of
course Ulrike's dad will ask Ulrike who I
am when he gets home, and he'll tell her I
was dancing with Georg, and Ulrike will
tell Steffi. That's just how things work. By
tomorrow morning the whole school will
know.

What Georg is really telling me,
though, is that he likes me enough that he
doesn't care what Steffi knows or doesn't
know. Or what the world knows.

Which is completely, totally cool.

So we go back into the reception hall,
and even though we don't hold hands or
dance so close we look like we need to get
a room or anything, we have a great time.
We're the only people under the age of
thirty on the dance floor, but it doesn't
matter.

And just when I'm thinking how glad I am Dad made me learn to dance like a proper lady, even though I've always been certain I'd never want to dance to anything like Mozart or Wagner or whatever it is the orchestra's playing, I catch his eye across the room. He's handing the minister of the treasury a glass of water like it's no big thing, but he's looking at me.

And he smiles. Well, until Georg's facing the other way. Then he's not. And it's *not* good.

I can tell from the way he very point-edly shakes his head that we're going to talk later, and it's going to be, as he would put it, a bit *unpleasant*. But he's beginning to warm to the idea of me seeing Georg, I can tell. He doesn't want me developing a smoker's rasp like Karl's, or hanging out in the palace men's room, but he wants me to be happy, even if getting to a happy place involves facing the risks that come with dating Prince Manfred of Schwerinborg's only child. That much I can tell.

Geez, at least I hope so. What if he's *really* ticked off this time? What if he threatens to send me back to Virginia over this? It's definitely possible. . . .

No. I won't think about that. I'll deal with Dad tomorrow. There'll be *some* way for me to get out of this. I have to. Because now I have a BOYFRIEND.

And I don't want to have to leave him. Let alone live with Mom and Gabrielle and deal with all the crap that's going to be coming my way from Christie, Jules, and Natalie.

Georg grabs my hand and spins me around, and I just can't help but smile to myself.

Who'da thought that my mom announcing she was gay could get me a boyfriend? A boyfriend who isn't a safety boyfriend, like Jason Barrows could have been, or someone like David Anderson either, who'd probably only think of me as his Armor Girl.

Probably.

Christie's my friend, so I'll let her say her piece, and I'll even make myself think through everything she has to say—I owe a girlfriend that much, I mean, hos before bros, right?—even though I know in my heart I'm not going to change my mind about Georg.

I cannot believe I have actually found someone who makes my stomach do flippity flops every time I look in his eyes. Someone who *gets* me and doesn't care if I'm popular or that my mother is a lesbian. Someone flat-out gorgeous who can kiss me inside out.

Someone who'll let me see just what it feels like to hook my fingers in the back pockets of his Levi's while he kisses me.

I can't wait to try that.

No matter what it takes with Dad, I'm so not going back to Virginia. This is where I belong.

Valerie Winslow never thought life in
Schwerinborg could be so great. But then
she never thought she would be dating
the prince, either!

What she doesn't realize is that things are
about to take a turn—for the much worse.
Prince Georg decides they need to cool off for
a while just as her dad decides to send her
back to Virginia to visit her mom.

Valerie's crushed—until she decides to go out
with her old crush David Anderson. David may
not be a prince, but he should be able to take
her mind off Georg for a while—shouldn't he?

Don't miss the princely sequel to
ROYALLY JACKED:

SPIN CONTROL
By Niki Burnham

★ *Available January 2005 from Simon Pulse* ★

"Once upon a time . . ."

is timely once again as fresh, quirky heroines breathe life into classic and much-loved characters.

Reknowned heroines master newfound destinies, uncovering a unique and original "happily ever after...."

Historical romance and magic unite in modern retellings of well-loved tales.

THE STORYTELLER'S DAUGHTER
by Cameron Dokey

BEAUTY SLEEP
by Cameron Dokey

SNOW
by Tracy Lynn

MIDNIGHT PEARLS
by Debbie Viguié